# I DREAMT THE SNOW WAS BURNING

by Antonio Skármeta

translated by Malcolm Coad

**readers international**

The title of this book in Spanish is *Soñé que la nieve ardía*. It
has been published in Barcelona by Planeta (1975), in Madrid
by Literatura Americana Reunida (1981), in Havana by Casa
de las Américas (1983), and again in Barcelona by Plaza &
Janés (1985).

First published in English by Readers International, Inc.,
London and New York, whose editorial branch is at
8 Strathray Gardens, London NW3 4NY, England.
US/Canadian inquiries to Subscriber Service Department, P.O.
Box 959, Columbia, Louisiana 71418, USA.

Cover and frontispiece: *The Fallen Goal I* and *II*, original
artwork produced for this edition by Nemesio Antúnez,
Santiago de Chile
Design by Jan Brychta, London
Typesetting by Red Lion Setters, London
Printed and bound in Great Britain by Richard Clay (The
Chaucer Press), Bungay, Suffolk

ISBN 0-930523-06-7   hardcover
ISBN 0-930523-07-5   softcover

soñé que la nieve ardía
soñé que el fuego se helaba
y por soñar imposible
soñé que tú me querías

I dreamt the snow was burning
I dreamt the fire froze over
And dreaming impossible things
I dreamt you were my lover

—from "Ay, ay, ay",
Chilean song

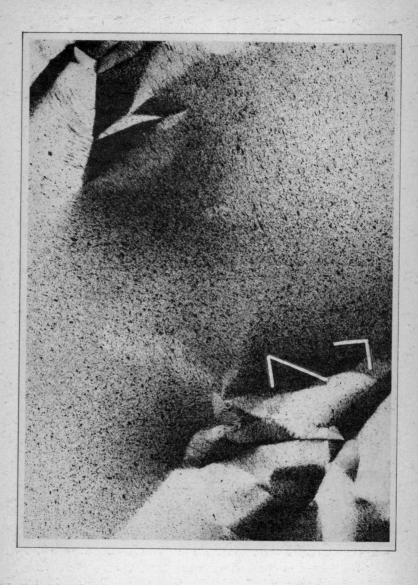

He slung the string bag behind him like a rucksack, and with studied irony surveyed the country around him. He took it all in: cloudless sky, rocks, wooden houses coloured like orphans' dresses, the huge horses. Passing the billiard hall, empty behind its green doors, he couldn't help a grin. There they would stay, endlessly caressing the same multi-coloured balls, dull from so much bouncing on stale greenish felt. There they would stay, the champions with their fruit shops, banks, taxis and receipts, bloated with beer, cigarettes and amorous bragging—above all, the insufferable bragging. He hung back a yard or two, relishing the rancorous admiration that would come over them when he, Arturo the kid, was no longer to be seen fiddling with his fly among the turks in the poolroom nor shining his shoes in the square for lack of pigeons or any other stupid creature to feed corn to, like a sanctimonious old woman; nor in the cafe watching '50s TV serials with their nubile, blind heroines and poor but honest doctors, the set as shrill as the expresso machine; nor at the matinees at the flea-pit, gob stuffed with peanuts, practising vain seductions on the princesses of the town, later to relieve his erections between private sheets. Prematurely, and confused with the noise of the drains and the agitated squawks of the birds, he savoured the sound of the coming train. The locomotive would approach furiously vengeful, saturnine, John Wayne in technicolour grinding across the main street with his bear-like stride to blow out everyone's brains with abundant lead. The train was coming for him, complete with firestack and billowing black smoke, worked up in the heat of the boiler; it would stop just there, at the point on the platform he had dreamed of, so that he, and he alone, could board.

"Let me tell you something, Arturito. If I had another grandson, he'd be my favourite, not you."

"Sure, Grandad. Let me carry the bags, will you."

The old man stepped away from the basket. "When the trouble starts you'll be far away, playing with your little ball. Instead of family, I'll have nothing to face the *momios* with but the teeth left in my head.* I'll tell you one thing, just so you leave knowing. You're my grandson because there's nobody else. Got it?"

The youth began to kick pebbles towards the ditch. "You're a pain in the arse, Grandad. Pass me the suitcase."

Their looks met, and the old man gripped the handles of the baggage more tightly.

"There's no help but you're my grandson. He'd be working here, with us. So there."

"You have no choice but to love me, 'cos you're my very own Grandad."

"Because I have to, I do. But I don't at all like what they're saying in town about a grandson of mine. Not at all."

"What're they saying?"

"That you've never had a woman."

"And you believe it?"

"If not, I'd have heard about it."

There was no reply from the youth. He tightened his lips, and held the ball in front of his chest ready to bounce it with both hands.

* *Momios*, derived from *mummies*, were those with "embalmed" ideas who supported the overthrow of Allende's Popular Unity Government.

2

"They're saying you should have made a start by now. That you go red when you talk to a woman. Red as a watermelon. I'm just repeating what they say."

"It'll be different in the city. Women there know what's what. Not like your thick-skulled peasants, Grandad."

"Watch your mouth! They're good comrades, game for work and for bed. And while we're about it, we'll see whether you join the Left in the city."

The youth tilted his head, feeling the lines of his nose and mouth redrawn already by an insolent pride.

"You're nuts, old man. All grandads get addled at your age, and start playing hell with their grandsons."

Reaching the station doorway, the old man put down the luggage, but without letting it go. He took a deep breath.

"Very well, Arturito. I hope things go well for you in Santiago. Or at least that you fall for a woman. Then we'll see if there's anything in that heart of yours—if only just the shadow of a feeling."

"I don't want any of that, Grandad. No everlasting love crap for me. Straight to the nitty-gritty."

"What is it you want, Arturito? What are you after?"

"The big time, that's all."

"All I hope is they make a man of you. Just like the rest of us, that's all."

Closing one eye, the young man sized up the distance between himself and the old man whose earth-grimed hands kept their post over the bags as if that deserted station were a den of thieves. He thought: grandads are like hogs; the older they are the more stubborn they get. But he said nothing, because with a soft glance the old man was gathering up the countryside around them, to offer him a last saw. As if a tree were also company, or a bird.

"Dawn's breaking earlier. When the sun gets warm by now, the days start getting longer. Breakfast tastes better."

It took no effort to imagine the old man alone an hour later, soaking pieces of bread in milk then sucking the milk through his broken teeth, while the hens pecked at generously scattered corn. The old man would kill his loneliness by eating.

At the other end of the platform, Arturo saw a tiny figure get up from a bench and, with nervous steps, move towards the track, as if in urgent need of the train. Even at a distance it was obvious that his thick black coat was generously oversize. Arturo pointed him out to the old man.

"A dwarf", he said.

The old man's brow creased as he focussed more precisely, then pronounced gravely:

"It's not a dwarf. It's a Small Gent."

"Whatever. When I get on the train, I'll touch him for luck."

"One of these days, Arturito, someone's going to sort you out good. And it's hunchbacks who bring good luck."

As the little man drew nearer, clutching his cardboard suitcase, his height and the unrelenting heat that was beginning to grip the station platform made his over-abundant coat seem ever more incongruous. He stood on tiptoe to see the train unimpeded. The old man covered the food basket with a cloth, and for the first time the young man took hold of the bags to try their weight. The old man approached Señor Pequeño and with a smile pointed out Arturo.

"This is my grandson," he said. "He's a footballer. He's going north."

Señor Pequeño looked at the old man, then immediately forgot that anyone had spoken to him. By now the train was pulling into the station, but he stood on tiptoe again, and once again clutched at his chest with nervous hands. The station master emerged in his vest, yawning widely, and exchanged a hand signal with the driver. He looked at his watch and rang a bell. When the train stopped, the town returned to silence, with only the steps of the two solitary passengers to distract the station master's gaze. Through a window, the old man gestured to Arturo to leave the seat he had chosen and move down two rows, opposite Señor Pequeño.

"Drink some milk every day," shouted the old man.

Very fed up, the youth rubbed the nape of his neck. The old man was preventing his enjoying this moment as he had dreamed and calculated.

"'Write to me!' Go on, tell me to write to you," he smirked.

"Of course, boy. Write to me."

"No need, Grandad. You'll read all about me in the papers."

"The chicken's to eat when you get to Talca, remember. And buy some boots for the rain when you arrive."

As the train jerked into motion, the old man stretched up, gripping the window frame, and addressed Señor Pequeño in a tone of desperation.

"This is my grandson who I told you about, remember? He's travelling with you. He's a complete virgin and plays football."

The little man glanced absent-mindedly at the grandfather, blinked at the youth, and buried himself finally in the contemplation of his boots. Vaguely he recalled having seen these characters on the platform

5

while absorbed in a daydream. The young man, on the other hand, exchanged his initial feeling of mockery towards the little man for the beginnings of disgust. Now, he felt, the curse of his virginity would pursue him all the way to Santiago, borne by this little man. At last, the train began to pull out, and the old man hung onto his neck and planted a rough kiss on his cheek.

"God bless you, my boy. You can always count on your Grandad."

By the time he let him go, there were already inches between them. Smoothing his hair with his hand, and stretching out his neck, Arturo shouted: "You're crazy, old man. First you tell me to comb it nice, then you grab me by the nut and screw it all up."

He waved a couple of fingers in response to his grandfather's extravagantly whirling hands, then quickly pulled in his own head and hand. As a result he missed seeing the red-headed man who approached his grandfather and, his arm extended horizontally at the height of the old man's shoulder, inquired about somebody. Nor did he see the old man nod his head in assent, nor the red-head, nodding in his turn, look after the train, which was now the length of a block away from them. Señor Pequeño, however, sitting opposite Arturo, back to the engine, did see them. To him the red-head seemed somewhat familiar. But why and from where, he could not say exactly, at least not without a shiver.


For a moment the young man had the impression he was on terra firma or, even worse, at home. A mixture of cackling and cawing clearly reached his ears. Some dawn bird, or fowl. The dust on the windows aggravated the smarting heat of an overpowering sun. The second thing which caught Arturo's attention, as he moistened his lips with his tongue and made brief flexing movements to adjust a stiff neck, was a certain commotion in the region of his neighbour's chest, which seemed a good deal more dramatic than simple palpitations. Somewhat intrusively he set about following the motion of the little man's eyes to and from his exaggeratedly agitated bosom. Having wiped his eyelashes with saliva, studied the fruits on the ends of his nails, and rolled them thoroughly between his fingers, he fixed his gaze on his companion's diminutive breast. Señor Pequeño, having unwittingly caught the youth's undivided attention, simulated interest in the flies hovering around the lamp above his head.

"I've come to the conclusion", said Arturo, "that you've got something in your chest." Señor Pequeño hunched his scanty shoulders even more, his body hollowing into a question-mark. "There's something there, isn't there? Something alive?" The little man scratched his cheek and began cracking his knuckles, pulling at them with the fingers of his other hand. "Look after it well, don't you?" Now the little man sat bolt upright, like a judge. "Must be nice and cosy in there, eh?"

Señor Pequeño pressed his lips together, perhaps wishing for a final dream to invade the train, the countryside and the tedious swell of the sun against his black coat. If only he could sleep, he thought, a thick cloud would lift him rapidly away hurling out thunder and storms in its path. The peasants would take shelter beneath mountains of wheat and he would travel, voluptuous but pure, within a familiar and grey space.

"Very well, then," said the youth. "If you don't want to talk, why are you sitting near me?"

7

His neighbour regarded the nearby seats and calculated how awkward it would be to shift his baggage while keeping both hands on his chest.

Arturo pulled the end of his nose onto the upper extremity of his lip, and waggled it thoughtfully.

"Not many people keep stuff in there. I don't know anyone who does that, actually."

"Don't you believe it," murmured Señor Pequeño.

"Didn't catch that." The little man pressed his knees together. "It's really strange, the way it moves about. Mind you, you're a pretty strange customer altogether." Arturo drummed his fingers on the leather of the football, then put it under his feet and began to rotate his hip. "Wriggles, eh? Something the matter with it?"

"It's like that."

"Like what?" He bent over and put his mouth very close to the other's ear. "A little animal, is it? Give us a look!" He pushed the small of his back deep into his seat and sat up straight until his head stood out high, pert and expectant. After fumbling a couple of times with the button, Señor Pequeño opened his coat slightly, and showed part of the cock's head. Before a second was up, he had pushed it back into his lap and, convulsed by trembling, slipped the button back into its buttonhole. Arturo stayed as he was, but rubbed the nape of his neck attentively. "Looks like a chicken, doesn't it?" Disillusioned, he took the cloth from the food basket and extracted a sandwich.

Before eating it he plunged his fingers through the fresh crust, making it split open sumptuously. Masticating a large chunk, his mouth open, he spluttered:

"Steal it somewhere?"

"No," said Señor Pequeño.

"But you've got it hidden."

"Safe."

"Ah. Because it's very nasty, that—nicking people's chickens."

He continued to watch his companion, chewing repeatedly in silence. After finishing the sandwich, he flicked the crumbs from his trousers as if scratching himself.

"Give us another look," he said. The little man hesitated, his finger in the buttonhole. "Go on, show it to me."

"It's for fighting," said Señor Pequeño. "It fights with its beak, and kills other birds."

"Could be thirsty, eh?"

Imprecisely, because of the swaying of the carriage, Arturo poured a little wine onto the lid of the salt-jar, and pushed it towards the bird's beak.

"Make it drink."

For the first time the little man moved an inch or two in his seat towards the youth. He submerged the cock's beak in the wine until it had drunk it all. Arturo withdrew the tin lid, and turned it upside down expressively.

"See! Now it's happy," he said. As Señor Pequeño started to return the cock to his lap, he stopped him with a gesture. "Let it get some air, man."

The bird set about pecking at the sandwich crumbs and the youth put his hand into the basket.

"My Grandad said to offer you something to eat. Are you hungry?"

"Somewhat."

"You're in luck today. I'm going to give you something to eat, okay?"

He broke a rosy-coloured chicken leg in two, and sprinkled it with salt from between his fingers.

"But don't get into the habit. After this, you'll have to fend for yourself." Señor Pequeño tore a piece of skin from the meat and with his mouth tiny and his

9

lips tight, began to nibble it. Arturo cleaned his fingers on the cloth.

"When we get to Santiago, you can return the favour, see." Señor Pequeño, absorbed by the tasty juices flowing through his slight stomach, responded with curt movements which Arturo took for commitment.

"Can you introduce me to women? D'you know any women in Santiago?"

"Somewhat."

Fleetingly, Señor Pequeño felt a sensation of touch, and pressed shut his eyelids in an attempt to make the image appear; but there was a yellow screen in front of his eyes, and doves that kept crashing into each other. He murmured something; he felt shrill as he extended a finger and pointed to a bottle of wine in the basket.

"Could I have a little of that?"

The youth followed the finger, fired off a grin, and winked in complicity. He uncorked the wine as he passed it over.

"Help yourself, go on."

He watched his neighbour's first, long draught, grinning again. Then he leant over and gently punched his knee.

"Now we'll see if you can return the favour in Santiago!"

Changing position, he snapped his fingers in front of the cock, making it flutter its wings. Señor Pequeño pulled again at the bottle, his pupils turning together in order to watch the level of the liquid drop.

"Great!" said the young man, and scratched the cock's back. "Like father, then bloody well like son!"

When they stepped onto the platform at Central

Station, the young man felt his body contracting and expanding like the steam engine. In his left hand he gripped the suitcase, while the basket dangled from the right, and after a couple of steps he found himself in the middle of a crowd of old women carrying bags with holes through which peeped the heads and necks of country turkeys. He stopped for a moment, and standing on tip-toe signalled to Señor Pequeño to follow him. As the exit drew nearer, he quickened his stride, ready to be dazzled by the city as he crossed the threshold. He pictured himself as an animal that had grown up caged in a zoo, and now at twenty was released into the jungle, in country which in one way or another he already knew from the daydreams of provincial siestas. But in reality the day was hot and overcast, the streets half-demolished, and the buses, passengers hanging from the steps, trailed thick columns of black smoke. There were no neon lights, nor did the streets curl into multifarious networks of motorways with cars chasing along at full speed. He propped the case against a wall, and squatted down, bewildered. Now he realized that all the time he had been expecting someone to be at the station to welcome him; but the Peruvian waltz over there and the crushing machine mounted on the pavement were a far cry from a resplendent band playing a welcome, all blue uniforms and gold braid. Señor Pequeño drew up beside him, also putting down his case and sitting down, and leaned his miniscule back against the wall, while his arms dangled between his legs like two sad fruit. Half an hour went by of a silence resembling stupor, or a nightmare, until the youth turned towards the little man and punished him with a look of disdain. The latter felt the impact, and set about grinding a cigarette butt into the asphalt until it was minced into fragments. The youth stood up and directed his gaze in the four points of the compass, taking stock in each case of the nearest landmarks and the flat horizon of two-storeyed houses with their fragile balconies.

"I'm getting pissed off," he said, and scratched his head frenetically. He contemplated the impassivity of Señor Pequeño, and gave the latter's suitcase a light kick to attract his attention. "Do you always talk so much?" Señor Pequeño transferred his gaze from one shoe to another. "Nearly all the blokes I've known have been chatty, good for a laugh. It's really weird you're not a bit livelier." He returned to scrutinizing the melée of workers, schoolchildren, street vendors, buses, planes reducing altitude as they approached the airport, and taxi drivers rejecting passengers by displaying their decomposing engines or flat tires, as if he were a strategist reckoning up his forces for a battle to take place nobody knows when nor against whom. "Right then," he said, without looking at his companion, "I could go this way, or that."

The little man cleared his throat and after wetting his lips with a little saliva spread on the tip of his tongue, stared straight upwards.

"I have just had a dream," he said. "I was with my parents..."

Arturo pressed his hands against his ears in incredulity. The violent theatricality of the gesture cut Señor Pequeño short, and he withdrew instinctively to the station wall.

"Don't tell me that now you're going to come out with some dream! Have I been telling you the story of *my* life, eh?" With desperate pleasure he scratched the item located between his legs and sighed deeply. "A man with some self-respect doesn't go around telling people his dreams. Just imagine if every time

I met anyone I started telling them my own personal dreams!" He collapsed onto his suitcase, and plunged his hands into his pockets. Then he crossed his legs, and ended by propping his head against the wall. "A dream-teller and chicken thief! Things aren't going to go well for you here in the city, Señor Pequeño."

The station forecourt was emptying as the grey and hot day closed in, infused with fumes from the buses and the smoke of the factories. There were no trains now, and the porters chatted in scattered groups, in monotonous abandon.

A '61 Buick painted like a taxi drew up a few yards from them, and out of it climbed a tall, robust man with enormously cordial teeth. He sported a brown suit with red stripes, and had spared no lather to achieve the silkiest of shaves, perfectly free of scrub or outcrops. Where his hair bordered his ears in dense spirals it was dashed with grey, like a mature gallant. He approached the pair determinedly, adjusting the voluminous knot of his violet tie.

"You gents from the south?" he said. Arturo regarded him quizzically from the feet up, glanced rapidly at Señor Pequeño's profile, and discreetly fingered the little bundle of money in the small pocket of his trousers. "If you need a hotel, perhaps I can be of assistance. Economic and decent. If full board is required, meals are modest but nourishing. What do you say, gents?" he finished, looking at the football at Arturo's feet.

"I'm a sportsman."

"We have entertained sportsmen at my hotel, and never a complaint. Players from the First Division, even. Ruben Marcos, of Osorno, and prior to that Ballet Azul, were all clients of ours."

Señor Pequeño stood up, and the owner of the

boarding house extended an all-embracing and solicitous hand. The little man took it and the other gave his a violent and friendly shake.

"I'm a variety artist," announced the little man.

The boarding house owner regarded his dress and baggage.

"I do artistic numbers, dances, impressions. I tell jokes. I've always had a happy disposition."

The owner assented by extending his arms in an almost religious gesture of welcome.

"You'll always find a friendly corner in my hotel, a place where everything is just so. Myself, without going overboard, I'm a singer by vocation and a poet by inspiration. What I do insist on, however, is the punctual payment of rent. On that point I am quite inflexible. I'm telling you this because many in the past have taken advantage of my good nature, see. But I'm quite capable of taking matters as far as eviction, I should inform you."

While the landlord was speaking, Arturo noticed that a neon sign advertizing Moletto shoes had come on in a barrage of stars.

"They never put athletes' names up in lights," he said, open-mouthed.

As the landlord looked up at the display, Señor Pequeño started suddenly, because the cock was trying to escape from its net. He slapped the bird down and pushed it to the bottom of the bag, tying a crude knot. For a minute the three of them remained there buried in their own respiration.

"Things in my life have been so many and so long," sighed the landlord, before an amorous sensation began to curl into the image of a woman.

Señor Pequeño offered no comment, though without realizing it he did step on the cock. The landlord lifted the bags and began to carry them towards

14

the car. As he loaded them into the back, he broke off
and embraced his two new clients.

"Three years singing with the European fleet.
Entire years on the high seas. Japanese subs under
our boilers. Hits at the time were 'Pretty Mariquita',
'Like This', 'Of a Sin I Am Accused'."

Arturo fixed his gaze on a distant traffic light.

"I need more speed," he said. "I don't get back into
defense quick enough. When I go forward, there's
nobody can stop me, see? But I lack spirit on the
return."

"Beautiful women on those boats, my boy. They
put real flowers in their cleavages. There was a flower
shop on board. Camellias, roses with the spines
stripped off. And for dances they put perfume behind
their ears and on their breasts. I sang Nestor Chaires'
numbers in a trio."

The young man didn't remove himself from the
man's embrace, but his eyes flashed sharply as he
stared at him close up.

"Can you introduce me to women? Any number of
women?"

"How old are you, son?" the landlord asked him,
holding him with a look.

"Twenty or so," said the youth. "Can you or can't
you?"

"Flowers and fruit on spring trees! To run your
hand over them, plucking them, peeling them, smell-
ing them. But I was almost always on stage, singing.
If you were to ask me, was it a happy time? I
wouldn't know what to tell you, lad."

"Dunno what you're rabbiting about. All I want to
do is lay 'em, gettit?"

"Nothing romantic?"

"Too right."

"Great athletes with their names in lights there

15

haven't been. But when Arturo Godoy fought Joe Louis in the United States, they put up a display, and the stars on it lit up and went off and moved about. They made a monkey out of Arturito. Great footballers I've known? Only one: Leonel Sanchez."

"I'm better than him."

"If you're better than Leonel, boy, then you're truly something."

"Don't believe me?"

"Sure, I believe you. Sounds wonderful to me. I've seen many things in my life. Like what, you say? Like a town wiped out by a volcano, or the drowning of transatlantic passengers."

As the car pulled into the Avenida Antofagasta and bounced over the uneven cobbles, Señor Pequeño's attention was suddenly drawn to a bar on the corner. Taking advantage of a red traffic light, he started to open the door.

"I'd like to get out," he said.

"Anything the matter?" said the landlord.

The little man probed for the handle, until he hit on it.

"Would you be so good as to mind the chicken and the suitcase?" he said, fixing his eyes on the street corner as if at any second fearing it might disappear in a puff of smoke.

He walked urgently towards the bar, and shielding his eyes with his hand tried to make something out behind the glass; but all he could discern was the landlord flicking through a newspaper. He crossed the road, and selecting the portion of ditch which best allowed him to observe the entrance to the joint, sat down with his knees pressed together, and his hands placed upon them.

He was still there when a piece of moon appeared and the first star flickered palidly, and the clouds scurried along propelled by the same breeze that turned over papers and pushed the rusty fruit cans. Señor Pequeño buried his forehead in his knees and tried to connect once again with the flow of his dream on the station platform. He replayed the first images in perfect order:

There was a perfectly white plain dotted with trees

that streamed milk, and polished, enamelled animals: green cows, golden bulls, blue horses. Señor Pequeño went from tree to tree, equipped with thick violet spectacles to protect him from the glare and carrying a clay pitcher, which he placed under the branches to catch the flow. Then he walked over to the well, where he had to wait for a man to climb the railings and hold out his arms to him. The man was his father. It wasn't that he recognised him as his father as such, but that a notice was hung on him which said in careful handwriting: *I am your father*. Each time the child went from a tree to the well, the animals gathered behind him, green cows, golden bulls, blue horses and turquoise hens all accompanying him. They grouped around him like bodyguards, then, as soon as he had handed over the pitcher, dispersed again and stood nearby stirring up the white foam of the plain with their lips.

At midday, the father climbs out of the well and the two of them sit on the log, while Señor Pequeño's father, a man hardly taller than himself and wearing garnet-coloured overalls and a green shirt, unwraps a packet covered in yellow cellophane and extracts several huge radishes, which he plunges into a packet of salt then presents to his son. The animals, muzzles placid and rumps relaxed, watch them dine in a silence so perfect that not even the crunching of the radishes can disturb it. Once the two have meticulously chewed the contents of the package, the father lights a cigarette and asks Señor Pequeño to sing something. Señor Pequeño crosses the plain and sings the lines of Osmán Pérez Freire: "I dreamt the fire froze over; I dreamt the snow was burning". He notices also that down his father's pale cheeks flow with discreet frequency a number of blue tears. He falls silent when he sees his parent rise from the log. As he moves, the latter's body begins to expand until it acquires truly monstrous dimensions and the seams of his shirt burst open crazily under the overalls like garnet flashes or flaming comet tails. The whole of space is calm but for the air that burns around his father, making his hair boil, while his powerful breathing causes his heart to beat explosively as if the entire world were expanding and contracting. Señor Pequeño feels a warm delight climb from his bare feet on the whiteness of the plain to his thighs, then through his sex and his heart and stomach, finishing like an intoxicated bird, forming a knot in his throat. Then his father pushes forward his shoulders, throws back his elbows, and, flexing his knees, takes determined flight into a space uncontaminated by clouds, suns or stars. Struck dumb and with neck outstretched, Señor Pequeño follows his father's flight, and when he is no more than an unchanging speck, almost motionless, walks over to the log, sits down, and begins to weep many blue tears, while the animals gather round him. Not that they are sharing his grief, but simply they are there.

At the moment he began to weep before the benevolent indifference of those sky-blue horses, the dream died on the spot like a needle stuck in the grooves of a record. With a shiver he felt the breeze in the Avenida Antofagasta and, upon opening his eyes, saw the back of a policeman who was directing the traffic. He crossed the road, taking care not to be seen by the cop. His eyes played over the windows of the bar, but it was too full now to be able to distinguish anyone clearly inside, and the few faces that he manages to make out meant nothing to him, while the backs curved over the bottles of wine were utterly remote.

He found a deserted table in the corner by the

window. Folding his arms on the tabletop, he waited for the waiter to come over, without once taking his eyes off the street, feeling at his fingernails with his thumbs.

The waiter bent over to take his order, then suddenly slapped his forehead with his palm.

"Señor Lecaros!" he said. "How have you been?"

"Round and about. Wine, please."

Searching the edge of the mirror for a glimpse of the landlord, he saw the waiter talking to him, then the landlord himself leave the cash register and come over towards him. Looking away from the mirror, he hid his face. He could feel the landlord's breathing beside him, and eventually lowered his hand until it came to rest on the rim of the table.

"How d'you do," he said, without looking up.

The landlord sat on the edge of the other chair.

"On your own?"

Señor Pequeño half emptied his glass, then wiped the edges of his mouth with the tip of his index finger.

"How've things been?" said the landlord.

"Well...", said the little man.

He swallowed the rest of the sentence, then took a deep breath. With his eyes fixed somewhere below the landlord's jaw, he drummed his nails on the bottle.

"It's been a while since your partner came around."

Señor Pequeño swirled the wine around without drinking. He didn't want the landlord to come to certain conclusions about him.

"I'm working alone," he said.

"Your partner left some bills. Like to see them?"

Señor Pequeño glanced towards the bar, then at the bottle.

"I work alone."

Closing his eyes for an instant, he caught just a

glimpse of the great herd of blue horses, and something else: his father's body, quivering in space like the trail of a crazy shooting star, until it was lost among so many other vibrations in the air. He called over the waiter, crooking his finger towards his own face.

"Where's the big fellow living?"

"He passes here sometimes, but without coming in. He's been seen in Quinta Normal."

"I don't understand."

"Playing a trumpet and collecting money."

"What's that?"

"An instrument. You blow it and it plays. Another bottle?"

The little man took some money from his neat plastic wallet, and held out one of the large notes.

"Give me another to take with me." He took back eight notes in change, then put into the waiter's hand another, small one which he pulled out of his trouser pocket. "Where should I go if I wanted to see him?"

"There's a boarding house in the street by the race track. A lot of people flop down there."

The little man stood up, buttoning his jacket.

"If he asks after me, you haven't seen me, right?"

"Okay," said the waiter. "How's the rabbit in the top hat?"

"Died."

"Little Pedro?"

Señor Pequeño noticed the wine was beginning to make his ears burn and that his legs were starting to sway slightly. Crossing in front of the waiter, he pushed open the swinging door, without saying goodbye to the landlord, and squeezed between the car bumpers, putting his hand to his heart to feel his wallet. As he slid along by the ditch nearest to the pale street lamps, he fastened the button protecting the purse.

When a startled cockroach crossed his path, he kicked it into the street with his heel. Only after checking there were no others did he push open the screen. An old man, his face covered with grey stubble, was knitting a shapeless scrap of wool. Beside him hung the Virgin of the Carmen against a blue background and flanked by a soldier, a sailor and an Air Force pilot. Señor Pequeño had to bend down to touch his shoulder. The old man grasped his knitting in his hand and made his way stooping to a small table where he opened the reservations book.

"You a cop?" he asked.

The little man wove together the fingers of both hands and with a single movement cracked the bones. The old man had put on a pair of pince-nez.

"No."

"Thief?" The old man poked out the tip of a bespittled tongue, and grinned, his tongue held between his few functioning teeth.

"I'm looking for a big fellow, about this tall."

With a brusque movement, the old man shut the reservations book.

"You a friend of his?"

"I have neither friends nor relations."

"Did he steal something from you; Have you got your police ID?"

Señor Pequeño furrowed his brows and, tilting his head a little, peered over the old man's head and down the passageway. It seemed to him that a young man clad in an undershirt was hiding in the shadows, and that now a hand was pointing outside and sharp left. The old man opened the book again.

"There are no rooms free," he said.

He ran down the list with a ragged nail, then lay his knitting down on top of it conclusively.

"Thank you," said Señor Pequeño, leaving.

"At your service," said the old man.

When he reached the corner, following the instructions given by the anonymous hand, Señor Pequeño stopped and twisted round towards the way he had come. The young man in the undershirt was in the doorway now, gesturing with his chin that he should turn leftwards. He checked the direction by waving a finger, at which the undershirt assented vigorously.

A few steps further on he discovered an entrance, smaller than a passageway but larger than an entry lobby. And there he found him, asleep on the pavement with his hands together for a pillow and his nose inflating with each snore above the dark flow of water in the gutter. Señor Pequeño circled around the mass of dishevelled and greasy hair, then withdrew a few steps towards the wall. Taking the bottle of wine from his jacket, he uncorked it and wiped the mouth. He walked over to the big man with the uncorked liquid, and placed it at a ready, but prudent, distance. Then he looked around him like a dog and walked quickly towards the front of the alley to see if anyone was coming. With some effort he tugged at the hair. A hank of it was soaked by the water in the gutter. For a minute he held the head in the air inches from the ground, but no change came over the placid composition of sleep etched into the most intimate weave of its facial muscles. Not unintentionally, the little man withdrew his hand and let the other's enormous head crash down onto the sidewalk. Observing the complete lack of any reaction, he could not resist giving the body a kick in the kidneys. He looked up, and above the overhanging tiles there was a miserable scrap of moon.

"Fall over, did you?" he asked the man. He looked from side to side. "Are you dead, partner? Is this where you're going to finish up?"

He put out his hand and pulled over a brick which fitted his backbone comfortably and precisely. He knew that as soon as he put his mouth to the bottle, the liquid would be annihilated by half. Nevertheless, he felt so snug and sure that with his eyes open he gauged the ration to make sure he did not exceed the already generous measure.

"A man like you should be working," he addressed the bulk, with animated cordiality. "What're you doing here, stretched out in the gutter? D'you want the dogs to eat you?"

He yanked the hair until the face twisted round towards him. His nose puckered as the man's face seemed to him to become paler and younger by the minute, the hair too firm, adolescent, repugnant, and histrionic for a man of his age.

"Despite everything, I'm going to offer you a job," he said. "For reasons strictly of my own I have decided to mount a show. I don't know if you still have any interest in show business." He prodded the other with his foot, without producing any perceptible reaction. Merely a more prolonged intake of breath and a scarcely dignified noise from his rear.

By the light of the moon, Señor Pequeño scrutinized what was left of the wine, calculating that now was the time for half the remaining half. He rolled a thick mouthful on his tongue, only releasing it on its way when he spoke again, frankly indignant.

"It seems you've never noticed that gutters contain water. That's what you want, is it? Gutter water flowing up your nose? Want to fill your nostrils with water, eh? Only corpses stay stretched out like that. Corpses have no scruples; they start to stink, and then...." He dug the big man's belly with his toe, and moved it about, pressing hard. "The garbage men will be along tomorrow, and they'll toss you into their cart." With his heel he attacked the other's kidneys. "Let's see how you like that. Let's see how you like that little outing amongst the rubbish and broken bottles." He put the wine-bottle between the other's lips, which formed themselves into a shape perfectly aligned with its neck. The little man tipped the bottle, and the liquid flowed unobstructed into the other's throat. "You like that, don't you? No problem at all, eh? Fifth rank artists! Crash out in the street, and never get up again!"

He withdrew the bottle a few inches, and the big man's hand, with perfect reflexes, rose to seek it out and pour the rest pleasurably into his mouth. Then the man opened a pair of wide grey eyes, closing them incredulously when he discovered Señor Pequeño beside him, before he attempted to embrace him.

"Don't say anything!" said the little man. "You've drunk it all. No manners and no decency. Do you want the job or not?" Raising his bulk onto his elbows, the big man nodded as if under a spell. "Don't think that because you owe me your life I won't pay you. We'll be partners. How's that?"

The man pulled at the nape of his neck, his eyes as liquid as a pool.

"How much?" he said.

"A percentage yet to be determined."

"That sounds okay."

"Then get up and try not to fall over again."

The big man sniffed profoundly, and began to move affectionately towards the other; but Señor Pequeño stopped him, palms outstretched and his body recoiling emphatically.

"You're very good to me," the big man had to content himself with stammering.

Señor Pequeño set off.

"Whether I'm good or not is beside the point," he

threw back over his shoulder, enjoying the protective presence of the enormous beast behind him. In the street now, they were like a child and an awkward Saint Bernard, leaving a trail of silence behind them as they passed the boisterous proletarian doorways. "The chicken's mine, and now to rehabilitate my partner," the little man thought to himself, quickening his nervus steps until he was almost running. He looked around him, then up at the other's face. "Our relationship is strictly artistic, get it?" He observed his partner's slight nod of assent, and added to himself: "It irritates me, that face up there". He lowered his eyes and laced his hands together behind his back without slowing his pace a jot. "An arrangement between professionals," he declared to the other, this time without looking round.

When the owner of the boarding house led Arturo into the lounge, gripping him proudly by the elbow, the youth's smiling gaze drifted among the flower vases with their fresh violets, the rocking chair where the old lady sat, her knitting wool suspended from between El Negro's teeth, and the piano, strings exposed to view, which Fats, grinning in desperation, was making vibrate impatiently, and he resumed the smile which he'd been rehearsing and gripped the football tightly as if it were a mooring post, and the photo in front of him was of the President with his chubby jowls and spectacles like a provincial teacher and proud dove's chest decorated with the tricolour sash, and beside it an image of Jesus about to keel over and another of frothy pink and blue ballerinas resting their little feet lightly on the bar and flexing their knees under butterfly-like tutus, and returning his gaze to the landlord, who was looking at the boys and hearing their shouts as if they were a chorus of angels, he tugged at his jacket, at which Don Manuel turned to him but only broadened his smile and winked at him to hang on a while, as El Negro went over to Fats, who had turned his back on him and was banging for all he was worth at an F-chord, turned him round to confront him full in the face and said to him no, man, that's a load of shit, you just don't get it because you don't have any historical perspective, that's your trouble, man, no materialist analysis of the objective conditions, see, teeth flashing under the 80-watt bulb and tongue darting from side to side when he managed to catch his breath, coming at him with everything, as sharp and unrelenting as a drill bit, first with his right, when you make a move, man, then with his left, you gotta know what you're going to do with your next move too, get it, man, because your problem is that you just up and say we have to get out onto the streets and face the bastards, then Fats: they're not bastards, they're fascists, man, and El Negro: so right they're fascists, man, and what're you gonna face them with, eh? the cops, is that it? 'cos you're certainly not gonna do it with the troops, not bloody likely; then we're well and truly up shit creek, Fats screams at him, now you've done it, Fats, says Carlos, and Susana, let him finish, Fats, yes, Fats, let me finish, says El Negro, 'cos what you have to see, what you have to *see* first of all, man, is whether the confrontation suits us now, 'cos if they're closing up the shops, stopping the lorries and coming out armed to the teeth it's 'cos they want a showdown now, and want us to go over the top, get it Fats, 'cos if they push us beyond what's legal, don't laugh you arsehole, if they push us beyond what's legal, they'll have the *milicos* up our bums like a shot; it's all this damn wanking blah-blah-blah that's gonna have them kicking us up the bum, says Fats, and El Negro, get this into your thick head once and for all, man, there'll be no shootouts, 'cos we've got where we are with the vote and the law, and oh, fucking marvellous, man, so all we have to do now is hand out little pictures of St Francis to the *milicos* and breadcrumbs to the birds, and don't fuck about with me, Fats, well you come out with all this bullshit, what do you think I am, born yesterday, you're an extremist, Fats, I'm no extremist, man, I'm just setting out the real problem, the real problem is who has the power, said Susana, really beautiful the kid with impeccable teeth and hips which aren't exactly bad either, who came out with the comment while moving towards the piano, and El Negro, they just need one martyr, just one poor s.o.b. who we do over in the street, and they'll come out with the whole totalitarian bit, murderers, the end of freedom, whether you like it or not, man, then they've got it made, yelled Fats, and came down with his fist on the piano keys, the Left doesn't even have the streets, we've had to give them up to the old women with their saucepans and fancy boys, for Chrissake, Negro, not even God Himself can forgive what you're saying, maybe (El Negro's turn now), but that's how things are, and we just have to keep up what we're doing, organising people in the neighbourhoods, security committees in the factories, voluntary work, that's all, our thing, what we've been doing, no Negrito, says the fat guy to him sweetly, I don't understand what you're telling me, you're chucking pearls before swine, Negrito, and they're gonna shit all over us because we haven't stood up to them anywhere, we did in the elections, said Susana, standing over them, oh sure, I know all about that shit (Fats), but that's irreversible, said El Negro, the people's consciousness can't be turned back, why don't you catch on once and for all that we have problems but things are going okay, Fats, we've lost the initiative, said Alcayaga, who had said nothing up 'til then and who sat twitching his knees as if they were electric, I don't like it, that's all, said Fats, ah no, Fats, says El Negro standing up and banging his fist against his palm, we're not going to discuss what you like or don't like, man, 'cos none of this was dreamed up by you, man, it's like it is and not how you'd like it to be, and if the fascists go into the streets and start fucking around then you'll just have to lump it, dear old Fats, because our line is democratic, old pal, and don't you laugh, you bastard, there's no talking to you, Fats, said Susana, but carried on talking to him all the same, saying if you get out of line, if you go outside what's legal, then you give the other bastards the excuse to do the same, don't you get it, and El Negro pitches in as well and adds that the bastards have the *milicos* behind them, man, not the popguns of your beloved extremists; I still don't like it, shouted Fats, not at all, if the doctors strike we have to let them if they close the shops we have to let them if they go on strike we have to let them they lie and kill and shit all over us and we have to let them, you know something, *compañeros*, this is more like a minuet than a revolution! And with his cheeks blown out, Fats snorts and makes a noise like a music box and sticks out his tongue and jumps into the air while opening his legs, all camp, and El Negro grins, and Alcayaga as well, while Carlitos, the taxi driver's son, thought there was no hope for Fats, that Fats was Fats, and he was a laugh, Fats, but no, said Susana, you're all screwed up (El Negro once again) read Lenin, man, and Corporal Sepulveda smiled, stubbing out his cigarette in a sea-shell ashtray, and Susana, if you want action, turn on the TV, while Mari, who hadn't said anything said as far as what you've been saying is worth it'd be better to watch TV, but El Negro had brought Fats' desperation to a head and he saw him all alone, corpulent, anguished, brave, driven to the protection of the piano by the machine gun of words, he saw Fats the worker, the first up on voluntary work days, the guy who won over the reluctant with his sympathetic way of explaining things, with his heart and a joke always on his lips, both of them more abundant in him than the air which he never seemed to find enough of to breathe, and so El Negro said, hang on a minute,

*compañeros*, let's cool down a bit, *compañero* Osorio
has a question, and (Fats insists) a disagreement!
softly, softly treads El Negro, okay, a disagreement,
and we're not going to attack or take the piss out of
the *compañero* because of a disagreement, he's the
one making trouble, said Susana, but El Negro, what's
more, *compañero* Osorio has every right to disagree
and make his point because he's the best and most
committed worker of all of us in the union, and Skinny
Alcayaga, give him a medal then, and Fats catches on
to the more edifying mood El Negro is after: look,
Negro, just say etcetera, okay, and El Negro is getting desperate because he looks to one side and
shakes his head and arm like a centre-forward who's
penalty kick has been blocked and who, on top of
everything, the crowd are heckling, and sets to work
with the only thing that's left to him which is to slow
down, make with that solemn, paternal and no-
nonsense tone of voice used for rounding up stray
sheep, now don't make things difficult, Osorio,
you're a good revolutionary and a good worker, Osorio, which makes you twice as revolutionary, so why
choose this moment to get out of line? what a surprise, eh! said Alcayaga (while El Negro smouldered
at him out of the corner of his eye), Fats out of line!
and Fats himself serious and hurt says how the hell
d'you not get out of line with these creeps pushing at
you all day, which made El Negro as happy as can be,
his face lit up, that's it, you've got it, you've caught it
by the balls, all joy now, you said it yourself Fats,
champion, man, that's just what the fascists want,
me tubby old mate, that all the sentimental fatsoes
like you should get all hot-headed so they can wade
in and mount a grand balls-up with the senators and
the deputies, and the *milicos* (chips in Susana), and
the *milicos*, rejoined El Negro, and your ultimate

international fuck-up with a full three ring circus at
the OAS and who knows what else, and then all softness and his eyes imploring, don't you see, dear old
Fats, that after all we've achieved just because the
bosses go on strike again and go into the streets you,
you man, Fats Osorio in all his glory, get all steamed
up and want to go out and beat the shit out of them,
want a full-scale civil war, all but, at the drop of a hat,
d'you see, *compañero* Osorio wants to wrap up the
whole strategy, and Fats just sitting there, hanging
his head: it's just that . . . and now El Negro is all calm
and cordiality, paternal, 'cos in the end, in the *end*,
now intense and no-nonsense again, it'll be the parties, man, the parties of the proletariat, man, that'll
decide the next step, and not a petty bourgeois like
you, oh no, none of that, Negro (Fats), I'm not having
that, man, we're all in this together man, and just so
you know (Fats still), just so you know, man, I'm the
son of a worker, man, and Skinny Alcayaga, right on
cue: you're too well-fed for a proletarian, man, and
Fats furious now, stroking the braids of Maria's hair,
like Mao Tse-Tung, man, or Nikita, and El Negro
going over to the piano brings his fist down onto it,
less fucking about, *compañeros*, and it's just that
moment, that precise instant, that the landlord
chooses to drag Arturo into the middle of the room
and say, children, let me introduce the new occupant
of the house, with everyone all over the place, glanc-
ing at him with about as much interest as at an ant or
a piece of fluff, how are you, man, and Susana over
Fats' greeting to Arturo continues with her there's
no need to be afraid of being called petty bourgeois,
Osorio, Mao and Fidel came from the petty bourgeoi-
sie for example, and Fats storing up all the breath left
in him: and Che, Che, man, after which with sweat on
his eyelids he scans the room, in the centre of which

Arturo and Don Manuel are still transfixed like two faded flowers, and El Negro summing up, for God's sake, *compañeros*, the important thing is whether *compañero* Osorio is in agreement with our strategy or not, and if he isn't, let's discuss it! and everyone chimes in like before, come on Fats, don't give in now, we'll be at this all night, for fuck's sake, and Fats, his hand continuously fondling Maria's delicious neck and even a little lower close by a pair of sweet, glorious and very dark breasts, what d'ya say? whether you agree or not that if the fascists go onto the streets we should stick to our own thing, Our-Own-Thing, and Susana and Alcayaga say yes, Fats, how long are you going to arse around, Fats, and El Negro fixing Fats with an unblinking gaze and holding the others back with his hand, let him make up his mind by himself, have you got it or not, man, once and for all, yeah, okay (Fats), agreed then? agreed, man, at which El Negro collects up his papers and distributes them among his trouser pockets, Sunday at nine, then, voluntary work, he says, same place as before? that's right, same place, and Fats and Maria go over to the landlord and Arturo, hands held out and shake his, all smiles and open house and Fats this is Maria and Maria pleased to meet you and Fats and the others are all from the neighbourhood, and Susanita comes over to shake his hand, and Maria let me introduce you to Susana, while El Negro comes up behind, how d'you do *compañero*, and Don Manuel opens his large mouth so you can see a golden tooth gleaming right down there at the back and with a finger winds the thick grey hair of his temples into distracted curls, until he can get a word in and says this boy is a foot-baller and everyone looks at him as if to say and so what? as if passing a suit in a shop window and going a little closer to have a look at the price, and in his

heart he feels the first stab of annoyance at the landlord for such a...a...*dumb* introduction, and he
squeezed the ball more firmly between his palms and
grinned, slightly raising the extreme left corner of his
upper lip, which was a smile he had practised in front
of his mirror in the south, and said, with his eyebrows
also slightly raised, yeah, that's for sure, I play football, at which the guys nodded their heads and the
girls smiled and the owner of the establishment
touched the ball, pointing it out to them as proof, and
then came a brief silence during which the youth
looked at them and waited to see who would ask the
first question and wondering what he would reply if it
was that sensational and pugnacious slim girl, Susanita with her small tits, but small like two large juicy
plums, Susanita who complained so much while
standing up but how would she be stretched out nice
and horizontal with him on top, eh? come on, come on,
and then, suspended from the silence, El Negro, inex-
orable and infallible from top to toe, and how about
your politics, then? and Arturo blinking three times
then about to say something, but Susana cuts across
him with her slightly husky voice, a thin chick it's
true but magic, and that's a fact, man, magic, saying
don't be so heavy, Negro, protecting me, the delicious daft bird, protecting me so these jerks don't
mess me around, and still talking (come-here-darlin'-
so-I-can-gobble-you-up-good), we're not sectarian
here, *compañeros*, with a friendly smile (friendly, but
not come-on, dammit), and just as Arturo is about to
speak Maria, with her face rubbing against the good
guy, Fats' jacket (some beautiful piece he picked up
for himself, the bastard, bee-yoo-tee-ful, for Chrissake!!) says, that's right, so long as you're on the left,
no problem, nobody's sectarian here so long as you're
on the left, giving the fat guy a jokey punch in the

stomach, that's the problem, isn't it *compañero* Osorio, and Fats, pretty groggy after so many rounds,
don't muck around kid, okay, and Susana (after sav-
ing me from the bullshit these turkeys talk), so you're
good at soccer, what team do you play for, and him,
none, see, I'm independent, right, I'm gonna see now
what team I go with, University of Chile maybe, or
the Catholic University, something like that, I'm
looking around, right, the best of luck to you says El
Negro, all fierce practical committed tactics and strategy and the kids looking at him meaningfully but the
cheeky swine carried on as cool as can be: on Sunday
we've a voluntary work day, want to come along? and
Fats: we have to collect scrap iron for the foundries,
old iron, tins, screws, nuts and bolts, cans, get it? and
Arturo looking doubtful, I'm not sure, maybe but,
and El Negro but what? I want to train every day,
Sundays too, and now Susana, ah, right, train with
the little ball, and what's more (Arturo) I'm apolitical,
and the silence now has nothing to do with the one a
few minutes ago which was agile and friendly, like a
bicycle, while this was a huge lump, dense as pastry
soup, and the damned word apolitical, as thick as the
head of a boa constrictor and with the tail of a worm
coils up in the silence, and although not repeated takes
over the whole silence which would have been more
than enough as it was but now Arturo really had to
put his foot in it, and after the silence and the gaffe
and the silence following on with his whole body, and
so in other words there's me over here, he spells out,
and there's politics over there, right? and as all of
them just hang on, he thinks he's fooled the defense,
that he wasn't offside but legal, purr-fect-ly-lee-gal
let's see it again in replay, and now live and in the
flesh, Arturo advances and says with all the gravity
of a news bulletin: d'you know that down south they

killed a peasant for getting mixed up in politics? got involved in defending the Mapuches and the farm owners came along and put a bullet through his head and afterwards they were let off with nothing, and the papers after said one thing then another and you never know who's right, down there it's my Grandad who gets mixed up in politics and he got riled up with me when they killed the guy, and I reckon he got killed out of stupidity, if you ask me, for trying to defend Mapuche land with nothing but sticks while the owners were armed, right, and he looks round at their lowered heads, all of them looking at the ground, the girls fiddling with their skirts and Susana adjusting a ring and only El Negro looking at him straight as if he were a statue in a public park, I impressed El Negro, made things crystal clear, seems like, so he won't be messing me around later, and El Negro himself put his hand to the back of his neck and Fats breathed deeply, and looked at Maria while the landlord's eyes shined at him accusingly, cheers, then, Don Manuel, and then El Negro, right then, see you, and Fats to Arturo with a final sad and desolate smile, be seeing you, and the landlord I'll be off too, while Susana goes on working at the copper ring, and all around her silence, the walls with their grey and blue paper, the bare light bulb and the clumsy piano, the President's photo, the calendar with a red date in May which isn't a Sunday, the chairs that don't match, the stained armchairs and the dust on the flower vases and the dogends in the sea shells and above all the rose and blue coloured print with the ballerinas whose little arses are fenced off by their gentle and so unsexy, so untittilating posture, their legs stylized and swans' necks like diaphanous fairies fleeing in the woods from dark executioners like the ones in the joke or from some gamekeeper endowed with an enormous hard-on.

Arturo rested the ball on his hip, and covering it with the arch of his left arm waited for Susana to stop fiddling with her ring and look up at him. He stared at her, and stared at her again, fixedly, until she raised her eyes, her face a little hurt but also patient.

The youth smiled at her with perfect naturalness. Lifting the corner of his lip and his eyebrows, and pointing with his free hand at the ballerina print, he said in a voice which emerged husky and agreeable:

"Degas?"

"I don't know if Señor Lopez points out there that I'm very bad on the return. I'm not much use in defense."

"He mentions it. He mentions it," said the trainer, picking his nose and wiping the result on his trousers. He glanced at Susana, who was flicking through a newspaper on a chair in the corner. "Is the young lady your sister?"

"She's a friend from the boarding house," he said, keeping his voice down.

Jaramillo stood up, rubbing his nose with feeling.

"Life in the club is very ascetic," he emphasized, with his finger on the letter. "No boozing, food in moderation, etcetera. In a nutshell, being a footballer is a luxury which brings with it a cross to bear. A champion is a man of steel, understand? You're young, and for the young many sirens sing. Many sirens sing," he repeated, moving his eyes behind his spectacles from Arturo to Susana. A smile fattened his ruddy and roguish cheeks even wider than usual, and he went over to open the door.

"Get dressed, Arturo, then we'll see you on the field."

With a single heave, the youth slung the canvas bag from his shoulder, and made way for Susana. The trainer took the boy's elbow and steered him towards the changing room door. Once he was inside, Jaramillo slicked down his mockery of a hairdo and, contemplating the young men shooting penalties into the goal, said to Susana:

"Now we'll see if this Arturito is as good at football as he is in bed."

Five minutes later, the lads practising tunnels and walls broke off, paralyzed: Arturo was entering the training area rigged out in the full colours of the brilliant, untouchable, can-do-no-wrong, glorious National Team. Feinting and dancing like a boxer, he made his way over to Jaramillo—who didn't like a bit, not one little bit, he said, the sneaky whispering behind his back which was aimed not only at the hero from the south who had arrived all dolled up like "Spring-bolt" Caszely, but also at blind old Jarami himself for having called in for a trial a kid whose head was puffed up high enough to scare off the birds.

"Okay, Arturo," he said. "Let me introduce you to our captian, Jauregui."

The youth made a non-committal gesture of greeting, masticating as if on chewing-gum, and Jauregui's hand was left outstretched.

"In this country we shake hands."

Arturo did so, and afterwards came Carrasco, 's'a pleasure, Vicuña, Bertoni, how d'you do, Charlin, Rivera, Etcheverry, cheers, Nomez, Franklin Martinez, Soto and Soto again, the first Soto's younger brother, a pleasure. Arturo was beginning to notice that here in the city he attracted silences like worms do birds, while when he began to talk people started to open up more than an accordion with a worn-out bellows.

"Right, then," said Jaramillo. "Our friend here is Arturo, from the south. Just to make matters clear, he's wearing the national stripe because he fancies himself, that's all. Selected he is not."

"I always use it," said the youth. "That way I don't forget where I'm headed."

Across everyone's features flashed an insidious,

silent, rodent-like and rapid smile. Arturo exercised his jaw as if chewing gum, although there was nothing inside but air, because he felt good.

"Friend Arturo," continued Jaramillo, "comes highly recommended by young Lopez, whom you'll have heard me mention. He's brought a letter of commendation, and it seems his speciality is attack."

"And free kicks."

"Very well. And where d'you like to play, Arturo?"

"Well, I play functional, see. Centre-forward, well down. The idea is that I loose off the ball from the centre and from behind, then drive down hard towards the goal. That's to say, I send the ball to one of the wings and whoever gets to it first shoots it back to me straight, see, trying to drop it more or less into the opening of the penalty area, and if it's a belter and low then all the better 'cos sometimes they put beanpoles in defense who can beat you to a header or get behind you when you're taking it in the chest, and that's the lot 'cos from then on I sort it out on my own."

The plan worked at the third attempt: Charlin runs, knocks it straight through and low, Arturo picks it up in the opening of the penalty area, dances round Carrasco, feints to the left and resolves to the right in front of Vicuña, and takes it through as if fixed to his boot, until right on top of the goalie and, instead of filling the net, cheekily deposits the ball just over the line, more like laying an egg than scoring a goal.

Jaramillo, who was refereeing, got nervous and began perspiring, until his glasses steamed up. By the time the ball was back in the centre of the pitch, all the boys from Flecha had come to the conclusion that they really had seen the play, and if they'd seen it, it was real—and the kid was ace. Jaramillo, meanwhile, couldn't believe it. He, who had seen his stratagems crumble at the feet of these crook-legged mules, about as graceful as moths burning themselves against a lamp, tree-trunks always playing physical, athletes with an eye on the main chance or iron-heads such as El Negro Campos at the beginning before the Fox had enticed him away and even took him into the glorious national team, Jaramillo did not believe it, could not believe it. The lad had made them dizzier than wine, dancing a *milonga* and leaping like a kangaroo, and all of it plotted like a mapmaker who traces his lines with compass and fine black ink, never making a blot, nor a crooked outline, nor a shaky curve. The little bugger in the tricolour gave the impression of dribbling along a knife-edge, like a tightrope walker who steps gingerly so that the vibrations don't break the jugs and plates, stacked all in a pyramid and spinning.

In his second notable manoeuvre, the boy once again sowed giddiness and reaped space, until Etcheverry decided to put his bony skeleton in action, and laid him out on the touchline. Jaramillo awarded the foul, and the boys faced Arturo with a five-strong barrier, though set only seven or so paces back. Unhurried, the youth positioned the ball precisely at a special point on the turf as if the centimetres of green were separated by whole countries. He closed one eye to gauge the angle, then before kicking off glanced at the others in the barrier, their hands guarding the family jewels and, gesturing with his right forefinger towards Susana, said: "That's my girl."

Then he took off, at the very instant when his foot drove force into the ball giving his ankle a twist. A current sprang from his foot to the leather, and the ball arched until it came to earth in Carrasco's net. The boys clapped and tousled his hair. Jaramillo came over to him, and Arturo tried to make out whether Susana had seen it, the presentation of his credentials, his introductory super-goal.

"Now you'll be wanting to know why I fancy a second division team and don't go straight for Colo-Colo, or the Catolica. That's what you want to know, isn't it?"

Jaramillo nodded, taking him to one side by the arm.

"You'll have your reasons, I guess."

"Too right. I want them to discover me in the neighbourhood team, and come and see me, so I can set the price. And I want you to train me in defense. Nowadays in football, everyone attacks and everyone defends, right? I want to be perfect. And I'm in no hurry, see?"

"Let's go to my office and work out a contract."

"Pay me what you can, without a contract or anything. I'll play for you, but friendly. I'll stay for as long as I want, and go when I want."

"I can introduce you to the First Division trainers later on. I could invite the radio to broadcast when you play."

Arturo gave him a slap on the back which knocked his spectacles awry.

"Wants his pound of flesh, the villain."

"Well, son, business is business, to be quite frank."

"We understand one another, Don Jara."

The sun had almost disappeared, but the sky retained a beautiful violet clarity and the damp earth a light warmth. The brush of his hand against his thigh made the youth aware, as was usual after a game, of the swelling between his legs. Smiling at Susana, he set off for the changing room for a shower, the ball hiding his pelvis.

Along the cobbled street stretched the light of the lamps, as they walked towards the bus, and Arturo took advantage of the timely shadows to breath the scent of the girl's hair, so close by. His bag hung on his back, and for a long block he rotated his hands uncertainly in his jacket pockets.

"Do you live near the boarding house?"

"Five blocks away."

"That's near," he said, unable to think of a single way to say what he wanted to say. He felt the bundle of tickets in his pocket, knowing that fatally soon they would reach the bus station. Susana walked with her arms crossed on her chest, and every time the light of a street lamp bathed her damp mouth her upper teeth shone, slightly separated, and in the delicate gaps the tip of her tongue appeared now and again, enough to drive you crazy. Arturo tried to distract himself by studying the design of the paving stones, but the whole young night spoke to him of warm earth, every doorway promised an adventure of mingled breath and swooning kisses, and his fingers buried in the cloth of his jacket intimated the marvellous dampness he would find between the girl's thighs, while his lips opened profoundly to receive her hot tongue, just as he had read in the favourite books of his schooldays. She had seen him play, had appreciated with her own sparkling eyes the music of his footwork, the admiration of the boys at the club, the trainer's relish. He was *someone*. What if he were to touch her? If he were to squeeze her arm and stroke a small and vibrant breast with the back of his hand? Would she let him? If he were to touch her ear with his burning lips, wetting it with saliva distilled from temptation, dreams, years of fever, years of envy of bragging schoolmates, heroes of novels and Hollywood actors. He felt his own swelling burn, while the more it hurt him the fewer devices he could think of. His hands, buried deep as he fretted them against the cloth of his pockets, were paws, his feet hooves, his mouth a dry and awkward muzzle, good to eat or bite with, but not for anything like placing a kiss on a young lady's mouth.

The bus had not yet arrived at the terminal, and the drivers were making ham sandwiches inside the shelter and drinking beer from bottles. The girl walked over to a nearby tree, whose foliage seemed to be projected onto her face, animating it with splendour and mystery. She saw the seriousness with which Arturo desired her mouth, and smiled.

"What's the matter?"

Given that everything, absolutely everything, was the matter, nothing less than everything about everything, he replied: "Nothing."

The girl blinked at him, slowly and intelligently, twice.

"Such a face!"

The youth shrugged, and pushed at the cobbles underfoot as if the ground were nothing more than a grovelling insect, a treacherous and slimy wild thing. He saw the driver climb into the bus, and arrange tickets and notes in the money tray. The girl made as if to move forward, but Arturo suddenly blocked her way, head on.

"I thought we might go to a hotel," he said, without looking at her, trampling the beast with his toe but also with his whole body, his whole weight.

The young woman opened her mouth, as if thinking or hearing through it.

"What?"

"A hotel, you and me." Susana blinked repeatedly without pausing, her face as blank and anonymous as a letter without an address. He saw this vacuum, and stared at her, repeating to her more loudly, almost at the edge of a scream: "A hotel! A hotel! Isn't that what you do in the city?"

"And why should you and I go to a hotel?"

The youth supported his whole weight on his two hands plunged into the depths of his pockets, until his nails pierced the cloth. What came out of his mouth was not what he had been keeping there, the sum of his knowledge, or intuition, stored behind the invisible circle of his own silence. Not even the look he hurled at her was his, nor the way he tightened his lips. But, at the same time, they *were* his. Confusion. That's what he was, and nothing more: a pretty lump of confusion. He should have boarded the bus, or begun to weep with his chin on his jersey. But instead his mouth, which was not his mouth, said:

"To fuck. Now that you're my girlfriend."

"Where did you get that from? How did you work out that I'm your girlfriend?"

"Well, girlfriend, *girlfriend*, no. Almost like my girlfriend, right?"

The girl opened her purse and took out two notes for the bus fare.

"Back there you told them all I was your girlfriend. D'you know how you feel when someone comes out with lies about you like that?"

"How should I feel?"

Now he was chewing his nails, feeling a red, sweaty weight on the back of his neck which wouldn't let him lift his face from staring at his shoes. She saw the driver was in no hurry, and put the notes back into her purse.

"Why did you say that?"

"I didn't like being there, in front of the goal, with no girl, gettit? I just thought it would be nice if you were my girlfriend."

"You just thought!"

"So I said it. I'm like that, okay?"

Susana leaned against the tree trunk, and looked at him hard, her mouth open. Her hips were pushed in front of her, and her belly curved forward, stupefied. Slowly Arturo lifted his gaze, until his eyes met hers, then briefly drew in his body, as if pretending to be a child. Tentatively, he smiled.

"Hey, Arturo. Are you really such a fool? Or is it just pretend?"

Cupping his hand, he gestured farewell like an animal scratching with its paw—then went for her breast. He felt it, without taking his eyes off her face. The girl stared at the fingers wandering over her, and her face tightened into a confused grimace.

"What do you think you're doing?" she said, without moving, her voice shaky, a little hoarse.

Arturo moved his hand momentarily from her breast, made a slow gesture of ignorance, then returned it to touch her again, looking at her calmly, but full of tension, almost ironically.

At that, the girl arched away from him like a cat, and pushed herself against the tree-trunk, frowning and leaving his hand suspended in mid-air. Then, bending down, she extricated herself from him, so that she no longer faced him and he had to let his arm drop as if it weighed a ton.

"Want to know what I think of you?" she said, softly and intensely, as if wanting her words to soak him as thoroughly as rain, drenching him, eating into him, impregnating his athlete's carcass, while he felt the weight of his empty grin, and looked away towards the bus. "I think you're a creep. That's what I think."

He couldn't see that her cheek was damp. He didn't touch it, and couldn't know that her eyelids were burning. He felt the friction of the brusque movement with which she took hold of her bag, and then her steps towards the running board of the bus. He didn't see her climb aboard, but went over to the wooden wall of the shelter, and from there watched her dry her cheeks with dabs of her handkerchief. The station manager blew the departure whistle, as the driver started up the engine. The vibration, so close by, seemed to knock him out of a dream. Sensing her presence as if she were still breathing deeply beside him, he heard her final words again, and suddenly the breeze disappeared: the air had withered around him like flowers on a grave. His gums were burning and his knees trembling. A cry rose from the pit of his stomach. But as it mounted his tongue, it would not come out. The righthand upper edge of his lip curled upwards, one of his eyebrows rose, and rocking his head cockily from side to side, he went up to the window of the bus, banged on its side as if wanting the driver to open the door, and said to her:

"All that fuss because I touched one of them! What would you have done if I'd had the both of them?"

Señor Pequeño ate without taking his eyes off his soup, as happens when strangers dine together. The big fellow, on the other hand, had swallowed his rapidly, with gusto, and only quietened down when he'd worn out the spoon and was weaving his fingers together between his legs to form a little basket.

Between the end of the soup and the arrival of the spaghetti, there was a pause in which there were no more forks left to move about, nor salt-cellars to rotate, nor bread crumbs to crumble with their fingers as if distracted. When the maid appeared with the dish containing the main course, everyone moved their chairs rapidly towards the table. Only Arturo stayed lolling against the back of his chair, poking at his spaghetti, and lifting it a little way towards his mouth, with no intention of eating it. Between the strings of pasta hanging from his fork he observed the big fellow noisily sucking at his.

Then the landlord said, clearing his throat:

"It's a great pleasure to make your friend's acquaintance, Señor Lecaros."

The latter nodded slightly, and cut into pieces a mass of spaghetti liberally bathed in tomato sauce.

"He's not my friend. He's my assistant."

"They call me the Beast," said the big fellow, pointing at his chest.

"And your Christian name?"

"Angel. But just call me Beast."

The landlord pushed his plate away gently, rested

his elbow on the table to support his jaw, and began to think.

"In my life I've known few men as big as you," he said, and the Beast interrupted his forking and amassing of pasta to stare at him, taken aback. "Eat up, please, feel at home."

"Eat up!" ordered Señor Pequeño jogging him with his elbow.

"All of them lovely people, with perfect manners and given to fine sentiments. In Oakland, to take just one example, there was one who had a neck like rock and used a cossack hat with ear-flaps. He did wonderful impressions of Bing Crosby." The landlord wound a string of spaghetti onto his fork and rotated it, returning it to his plate. "What tall women have I known? Few, but all faithful and very hygienic. I married one once in Sweden. We minded a hat shop, and whenever it was hot I took shelter under her as if under a shady tree. A tree with ants, to be sure, because I used to tickle her a lot." Arturo looked at the landlord and winked. The latter stared at the wall, and turned the palms of his hands upwards. "I don't recall how life parted us," he said.

They kept a minute's silence, full of feeling, only broken by the Beast's clumsy scraping of his cutlery against his empty plate. The landlord inhaled deeply and struck the tablecloth.

"Speaking of Rome, gentlemen," he exclaimed indignantly, "it would be an idea for some of you to pay your rent. I withdraw my confidence from no one in particular, nor in general, but it would be an excellent thing if some of you would pay up. Money, if you get my meaning. I've observed, Señor Pequeño, that few in this establishment work. And where there's no work, it seems to me, there's no cash. And where there's no cash..."

"I'm rehearsing a new miming-to-records routine."

"Excellent news! So long as you're not too perfectionist about it."

The Beast wiped his plate with a piece of bread. "Señor Pequeño has a plan to make some money," he said. "He's the owner of a chicken that pecks at other chickens and kills them. We're gonna make it fight other chickens and make money."

"Why don't you shut your mouth," the little man said to him in an undertone.

The Beast pointed a finger at Arturo. "He knows the chicken well." Everyone looked at the youth, but he only threw a nibbled piece of bread onto his plate.

"I don't wanna get involved, all right?"

The landlord stood up and, supporting himself with his hands on the table, announced;

"I need you to pay me soon. No afters or coffee today."

He went over to his favourite chair to read the paper, tuning the radio to a programme of sports commentary. The Beast whispered to his partner:

"Did you see he didn't charge me? He didn't even realize I was here. I went unnoticed."

Señor Pequeño pulled at his forehead, almost to the point of scratching it. "All right, all right. Now keep quiet."

Arturo flicked a breadcrumb, which bounced on Señor Pequeño's lapel. Before speaking, he sought out the latter's gaze. The little man was calmly picking at one of his gums.

"Chicken thieves end up hunchbacked," he quoted, adopting an accelerated but confidential mode of speech, to which Señor Pequeño responded by stretching rearwards against the back of his chair. "I don't like thieves. And I don't like cheap performers. Just watch it, Señor Pequeño." He leant back a little to allow his eyes to flash above the little man, and then latched onto him again. "Above all, I don't like people who don't keep their promises." He ruffled his hair furiously, and turned his attention to the head of the table where Fats was slowly consuming the remains of his spaghetti while absorbed in reading a book. Lifting a fork with two fingers, he banged it against a bottle. "It's bad manners to read at the table."

Fats bestowed a wink upon him, turned the page and carried on, content as ever. Señor Pequeño elbowed the Beast, and they got up and filed out towards the staircase. When they had gone, Arturo wiped his mouth with his napkin.

"What are you reading?" he asked Fats.

"Lenin."

"The twat who says we're all the same?"

"He doesn't say that. He talks about how to make a socialist revolution."

"Socialists want us all to be the same. I know that from school."

"They want the means of production to belong to everyone. They've never said we're all the same. Are you interested in finding out?"

"I don't like politics. Just want to live with no problems, making trouble for no one and no one making trouble for me."

"So nothing changes? The same injustice?"

"Is that my fault?"

The door was pushed violently open, and through it came El Negro, Alcayaga, Susana and Mari, wearing paint-splashed overalls. They set about spreading newspapers on the floor and putting tins, paint and brushes down on top of them.

"They've come out with it," said El Negro. "They want the expropriated factories to be handed back to the owners."

Fats slammed the book down on the tablecloth, and looked at Arturo.

"Class justice! That's what it says here, son! What are we gonna do?"

"The workers are organising to defend the factories. We're going out to paint slogans. Put on your overalls."

As they gathered together in a corner of the room, Arturo went over to the piano. Taking out a handkerchief, he began to dust the keys. Corporal Sepulveda also got up, and went out towards the street. A minute later, Susana went over to Arturo, smiling.

"Wotcha."

"Wotcha."

"Angry?"

"No. It was you that was angry."

"The things I said about you afterwards!"

"Oh yeah."

The girl pressed a couple of keys, suggesting the first notes of the Left's anthem. El Negro and Fats applauded exaggeratedly from the corner. As she played, her head low, Arturo eyed the irresistible gap between her breasts. Then turning away he rubbed and rubbed at an impeccably clean black note as if it were covered with a layer of mould.

"Want to come with us?" asked the girl, observing his meticulous labours.

He carried on rubbing, blushing slightly, and by now quite incapable of looking at her.

"Where?"

"Painting. Seeing as you're on your own all the time, I thought you might like it. And it'd be a help, just in passing."

"No, thanks." He swallowed all the saliva which had been accumulating at the back of his tongue and stammered, without conviction, defeated in advance,

"I'd like to go out with you alone. To the flicks."

"Another day."

"Why not tonight?"

"Tonight I'm going out with them. Tonight we're working with the people, get it? That comes first."

Arturo felt as if a spring, fixed in his stomach, was forcibly lifting his head. He bit back his words, so only she should hear them, his breath rent, as if by a silent belch.

"You go around all mixed up together like animals. One behind the other, sniffing each other's arses. You can't be apart from them for a moment, even to go to the flicks. You get scared without them, you're nothing, ain't that true?"

He grabbed the piano lid and shut it with a crash, then opened it and shut it again until the landlord felt obliged to look up from his paper. He tried to calm down, but it seemed to him that the air was flame, and he was one of those con-artists like Señor Pequeño who swallow shit and fire in the circus. He dried his hands on his thighs.

"I'm getting out of this *pension*! I'm going where there are people who know how to live, who can communicate with me! Who have personality, a bit of style!"

In a second, the girl altered her immediate reaction to one of distanced irony.

"You mean you want to go somewhere where everybody spends their time drooling over you. D'you know what your problem is, Arturito? You have a navel this size! You're a guy who spends all day long contemplating his own blessed navel."

"I've got friends in other places! There are other friends I can live with!"

As she turned her back to him, Arturo grabbed her brusquely by the elbow. Breathing unevenly, dizzily, he whispered very close to her ear: "For Chrissake, don't you get it, I love you!"

The girl saw his mouth trembling, his cheekbones hot, the dirty shirt collar against which protruded a purple, palpitating vein. For a fraction of a second she thought the youth would hit her, crushing his twitching hand against her nose until it bled. But she held back the cry that was on the tip of her tongue, and once again interposed between them a delicate calm which accentuated and pinned down like a dead insect the spectacle being offered by the youth. She took hold of the hand which pressed into her, and tried sternly to push it away.

"So what am I supposed to do about it?"

The lad's eyes opened wide, bathing him with a look of shipwreck, the absurd logic of the innocent:

"You have to love me too!"

Susana contained her smile, because the irony on her lips had given way to confusion. It seemed to her that rather than a scene she was living in the flesh, this was a chunk of dialogue from a film she'd seen sometime as a child. Featuring Los Tres Chiflados, perhaps. After three soft slaps on the hand which gripped her, she managed to free herself. But she stayed beside him, feeling mature, dangerously wise. She didn't like herself when she said, like a schoolmarm:

"And what's so special about you that I should love you? Do me the favour of telling me that, if you please."

The question made him blink, grinning with sheer incomprehension. His flabbergasted astonishment was in his sagging shoulders, the curve of the small of his back, the trembling down on his upper lip, the vibration of his nostril. He looked up, and saw the tranquil scene around him: a group of people mixing paint and soaking dried-out brushes, a policeman who crossed the hall towards the staircase, a man reading the newspaper. So he simply swallowed.

"And what's so special about Fats? Or the landlord? Or Chico, or the Beast, or El Negro?"

Susana tilted her neck, and her head dropped a little, almost onto his shoulder.

"Warmth."

His hand went to her wrist as clean as a knife.

"And me? What about me?" he said, then suddenly, in a flash of inspiration, lowered her hand towards the bulk of his sex. "Just feel me down there, then."

"Let me go," she said.

Arturo eased his grip. The others had just managed to hear the last few words, and were no longer working. They were watching them now, and El Negro got up, alert. The girl crossed in front of them and went out towards the street. Arturo shammed a smile, letting it slip away as the others turned back to their tins of paint. Then he walked over to the landlord, and turned down the volume of the radio.

"Don Manuel," he said, "I'm a virgin."


Señor Pequeño was extremely punctilious in his dress. Each time he conceived a new idea, he liked to go over to the wash basin in the room, wash his hands, and then clean out the contents of his nails with the points of a pair of scissors. Lately he had become the fanatical wearer of a carmine dressing gown with gold filigree, the only item in his wardrobe which was not only worthy of an artist, but possessed the rare virtue of being adjustable to his size. Within two weeks of his arrival, the economic strategy was laid: the Beast would take charge of the bird, for which he showed a special affection, while he would poke around in his showman's valise until he came up with the perfect props for his new routines. As far as his art was concerned, he saw himself as a practical man: he allowed his imagination to venture no further than the limits of his possibilities, although towards midday one notion did lead to another and he permitted himself some flights of fancy that would have required an apparatus like that of the Folies Bergère to bring them to fruition. Soon, however, his indulgence towards his own dreams disgusted him, and from then on bad temper illuminated him like the halo of a saint. With his head propped against the pillow, he became aware of the Beast playing with the cock on the floor, pursuing it with the marionette Cristobita from his former "Big Head Show", based on texts by Garcia Lorca. He extracted a bag of corn from the bedside table, and signalled to Angel to come over and get it.

"Give the chicken something to eat." His partner picked out several grains, and rubbed the fattest between his thumb and forefinger until they shone. "Give them here," insisted the little man, cupping his hand so that the Beast could put the grains into it. Lying on his stomach on the bed, he hung over the edge and the cock hurled itself at him, excitedly. It pecked precisely, until finally it buried its beak in his hand to the bone.

Señor Pequeño dealt the bird a blow that knocked it to the door.

"Once again it went too far," he said. "Give it something to drink."

The Beast tried to tempt the fowl with a little bowl of water, delicately held between his cigar-like fingers.

"Puss, puss, puss!"

"Don't be an idiot! Don't call the chicken as if it were a cat."

The bird only approached when it saw a few grains of corn floating in the dish, and polished them off with precise pecks of its beak.

"He's feeling better today," said the Beast.

"Now dunk some bread for it. It likes that. And do us the favour of not drinking the chicken's wine. Is that clear?"

The Beast obeyed, except for a trickle dribbling down the side of the bottle, which he attended to with a hygienic lick of his tongue.

When the telephone rang, confused with the cawing of the birds outside, Señor Pequeño leapt from the bed, and tightened the belt of his dressing gown.

"Hear that?" he said. "It scares me."

He indicated the cock, as of swiping with a sickle.

"Put it in its cage."

The Beast closed the fowl in its wicker basket and went over immediately to stand by the door, as the staircase outside creaked under the strain of powerful strides. They vibrated in the glass of the door, which was soon pushed open discreetly by Don Manuel. Seeing them waiting each side of him, the latter couldn't resist feigning astonishment at his lodger's *robe de chambre*.

"Lovely smoking jacket, little fellow. Run up by whom? General Electric?"'

"The Cosas Company," he replied.

"Attire like that you don't see every evening. I remember one in the 'thirties that would give it a run for its money. But don't worry; it was in a film and was used by Ronald Coleman. It certainly suits you."

"Thank you."

The landlord bumped against the prop box, which he regarded with relish, his glance then alighting on the puppet which the Beast still had skewered on one of his fingers. The big man lifted it up, and made it gesture melodramatically with its arms. Don Manuel scratched his cheek.

"There are more lodgers in this room all the time," he said. "I came to tell you there was a phone call."

Señor Pequeño tightened the dressing-gown at the waist, keeping his hand firmly against it as if fearing that some booty might escape through its folds.

"The telephone," he said.

"They asked for a small person. A man. In a black suit. If he was a lodger of mine. Unpleasant sort of voice."

He bent down, and picking up a grain of corn catapulted it with his thumb into the wicker basket. The cock gobbled it up, his sharp eyes seeming to be expecting more. The landlord stood up again and opened the prop box. Unable to resist, he picked out a black top hat, and plunged his arm into it, right through the broken bottom.

"The rabbit?"

"Dead."

"So I see. As I was saying, a very unpleasant sort of voice," he repeated, rotating the hat on his arm. "I told him no, I'd never seen anyone of that description in my *pension*." He dropped the hat into the box, and prodded the little man repeatedly in the chest with an admonishing finger. "Get hold of some money. I can't wait much longer, understand?"

He opened the door, winked at each of them, and lightly tapped the latch.

"Would they have been asking after you, Señor Lecaros?"

"I have never spoken by telephone."

"If you've never spoken by telephone, then they could hardly have been calling you."

"That's what I meant."

"Very well, then."

When Señor Pequeño heard his host descending the stairs, he undid the knot of the dressing gown with a nervous twitch, and pulled it over his head with a single tug. Going over to the mirror, he knotted his tie, his eyebrows and fingers dancing a tango. With a gesture he ordered his partner to attend to the cage, which the latter lifted while Señor Pequeño set about covering it with a newspaper until the cock was only perceptible by the flapping of its feathers, like a ghost. Donning his black jacket, Señor Pequeño positioned himself under the light bulb, as upright, diminutive and rounded as an exclamation mark, slicked his hair and indicated to the Beast to pay attention. He turned full circle like a mannequin in a shop window.

"How do I look?"

"Very good."

"Impeccable?"

"Impeccable, Dad."

"As for you, I'd be grateful if you'd wash your hair with soap, and this week, if possible. There are odours in this room."

"But my cold, Dad."

"Between dead and dirty, I prefer you dead."

He indicated the door as if pushing a bell. The Beast opened it, waited for him to pass, and followed him, locking the door behind him.

Everyone as happy as can be, crammed like sardines in the bus, blowing on the comb-and-paper, drumming on the seat backs, a grand matchbox *marimba*, concert of snapping fingers, nothing patriotic about the thing, all of them like drowned rats in the freezing dawn sun, but all of them happy, as if it were the beginning of the holidays not work, work, work and toil, 'cos that's how things are in this country, they shoot at us and we carry sacks, they burn down our meeting places and we go out to irrigate the countryside, they're gonna shit all over us with a coup d'état so we go into the streets and put on the best march you ever saw and I reckon that when we all get together in the Alameda who the hell is gonna move against this people, who can stop us bastards, if we're all together, every last one, on the march, and you think, those who are against us like that, those who fuck us about, those who strike and cut off our food supplies and have us so deep in the shit, why, you think, can't we just stop their game dead, and the truth is we've the lungs to work at whatever we have to, we've the backs to put into it and the voices to shout with, but shooters I've only seen in the flicks and bullets only in the *compañeros* they kill at night, but we're unputdownable, like Alcayaga said up 'til last night, and now here we all are happy, unputdownable, dearest old skinny bosom-buddy, you've collapsed on us so early in the morning like a sack of spuds, you who were the only one of us who hit the sack early last night not like all these *compañeros* here who have come to work with their silly litres of *cuba libre* and more stale with ciggies than a poor man's dog-end, you who are the king of the songs by Quilapayun and Jara and Payo Grondona, and that woman you like so much, tell me you're laughing inside your overcoat, me skinny old mate, get the song, Skins, stop-them-for-sure, stop-them-for-sure, says-the-voice-of-the-people, Salvador, stop-them-for-sure, stop-them-for-sure, sure-we'll-stop-them, the-conspirators, that song, *compa* Alcayaga! and stop crying for Chrissake can't you see you're depressing me and if I get depressed the day'll go down the pan 'cos it's God's law that all us Fatsos have to be great for a lark 'n' all, a depressed Fatso's good for nothing, like a pig at mass, I mean you can spend the whole day with your face as long as a wet week, Skins, but if I leave off smiling just for a second it's what's the matter, Fats, from all the boys, are you hungry, Fats, tell me you're not crying, Skins, and there he is crying all over my shoulder; I'm not crying, Fats, yes you are, man, and Skins, I don't want the kids to realize, and Fats: shit, as cosy as we are they're gonna think we're queer, gotcha, Skins, you laughed, and Skinny laughing and crying, sure I'm laughing, Fats, then he's crying again: what's the point of living, Fats, what's the point of it all, all the argy-bargy and the blah-blah-blah, if it all ends with a bullet, Fats; shit, *compadre*, don't go philosophical on me, leave that stuff to the kids at the university, get the song it's-the-voice-of-the-people, Salvador, stop-them-for-sure, and outside the cobbled streets of the city and the Alameda deserted and the newsboys saluting with their fists in the air and the street sweepers with their fists in the air and the old women dressed in black walking to mass indifferent and all scornful because there are shortages of sugar, shortages of oil,

61

shortages of God knows what, syrup, deodorant, and a litre of oil can be got for a bullet; yeah, come on Skins, pull yourself together, man, and Skinny: I can't, man, I can't; my life, what a cry-baby, Skins, and the song stops and none of the buggers have anything better to do than chit-chat about what's happening in the rear seat and Mari in person leans over, her face pale, and just has to point out Skins doubled up and his claws buried in my shoulder and me holding him closer and closer because of course all the tears had to fall onto Fats' belly, and for Chrissake my shirt's as wet as this little country which is heading for socialism by the peaceful road, and Maria: the peaceful road, Fats, the peaceful road means they're gonna chuck us all in the Pacific; belt up, Mari, the more you talk the more he cries, and Skinny himself for the first time raises his face from my breast and lifts his green eyes towards Mari and I see that face and for Chrissake where did my dear *compañero* Alcayaga get that face, shit the feeling it gives you, a snotty handkerchief Skinny's face, scraps on a plate in a restaurant Skinny's face, and Mari can't bear to look at it and throws herself on top of him and on top of me too and as the daft girl's good for a weep as well she grabs Skins' hair and squeezes and squeezes as if to press all the tears out of him, and just to make the whole mess worse begins to blubber as well on top of his head and now all the kids in the bus have realized what's going on and stare at us blankly and a little guy gets up and says I'm from the Medical Faculty *compañeros*, and the *compañero* has a doctor's face, blue eyes and a kind of duffle coat, I'm from Medical, Osorio, and it's okay, *compañero*, I say, this is a sentimental matter between *compañeros* which is none of our business, okay? and the girl nearby gets the message and begins to sing that other thing by the

Quila, "How times are changing", and the kids, good
for them, catch onto the rhythm and take it away
with gusto and never mind the sleepless night I'll be
seeing them all day long in the onion peeling shop on
the Panamerican Norte, job humping sacks, job separating the rotten ones from the good so they don't
turn them bad, job loading them onto the lorries, job
shifting them to the Almac supermarket at Santa
Julia that we expropriated from the crooks, and hell
the good feeling that rises in my throat when I think
of all the geezers who are leaving home this Sunday
to go and work, job grease to your elbow stout heart,
job sing, and down the drain goes the Sunday morning neighbourhood soccer match, the doze between
tepid sheets, the morning toss with the *compañera*
arse and back good and warm, ravioli and spaghetti
round at the grandad's with a lovely red vino to help
them down, entertainment down the tube, nothing
but cold in the warehouses loading and unloading,
nothing but work your balls off down the mines, in
the textile works, in the shantytowns, in the schools
setting up supply centres, get the spirit, Skins, look
at all these buggers, who can be a match for them,
we're invincible, Skins, there's more of us, man, and if
they've killed our Rucio Ahumada we'll become more
and more so Rucio will grow too, Skins, 'cos now
Rucio's dead all the buggers everywhere know they
have to fight for what Rucio fought for, it's as though
there were a million more Rucio Ahumadas, and
Mari: that's right, Fats, that's right; and Skinny
crying: I dunno, Fats, you know how to talk pretty,
Fats, hell there's nothing shittier than a thin man
weeping, sobs bouncing through his body like a current, and they go all electric these weeping skinny-
limbs, seems like they'll die when they weep, sobbing
as if electrocuted, calm down Alcayaga, and Mari:

63

take this hanky, go on, and Alcayaga takes it and uncorks his face from my chest and sits up dead straight in his seat and with Mari's handkerchief wipes the whole of his face as if the hanky were a towel and inhaling long and deep looses his whole body in a final full-bodied hiccup, and when he removes the cloth from his features looks as calm as the Pope, lights up a Richmond, which he's smoked since he was fifteen, and smiles at me, smiles at Mari, and smiles at all the kids in the bus who are whispering in his direction, smiles as if to say the show's over, *compañeros*, shit Fats, he says, a goddamned soap opera we had back here, then, you gave it all its colour, I tell him: yeah, seems like I never stopped, eh, Fats? shit, the truth is I don't know how you didn't drown with all those tears inside you; better that I let them all out once and for all, eh, fat man? too true, and d'you know what upset me most of all, Fats? no idea, Skins; what upset me most of all was when the Commission went to tell Rucio's wife he'd been shot, d'you know what it's like, Fats, to be at the front door of the house with your finger on the bell and not knowing which of the four is going to say it because none of you has said anything, all of you staring at the ground? how could I tell the *compañera* they'd killed Rucio on a march, that they'd shot him in the middle of thousands and thousands shouting, and when she asked, why? what was I going to say, Fat Man, and that's when I began to cry, Fats, only not a tear came then, and I heard Rucio's baby's voice inside, and for God's sake *compadre* I wished that bullet had killed me a thousand times, and the oldest *compañero* rang the bell and inside were the *compañeros* from the Party, they already knew everything, Fats, they'd already told them everything, and the words which I'd not even thought of stayed stuck in my gut, stuck there like a bullet; sure, Skins, now we have work to do; and Alcayaga grips me hard by the arm, grips me like you'd grip your brother or your mother and says just one thing, tell me Osorio, and tell me from deep down, from the balls, tell me if you really believe this thing is gonna be sorted out by working, that we're gonna win out with voluntary work and marches, that's all I want you to tell me, brother; and I, Fats Osorio, looking at all the *compas* there, pooped from being up all night, hair long, noses dripping, eyes bleary and as sweet as lakes, and the girls with their knee-length socks and thighs under their mini-skirts white with cold, sharing out coffee from a thermos, I, the most ultra Fats ever known not so much for the ideas in my head as because my heart was always further to the left than all the rest, although it brings me nothing but hassle and every week the shit beaten out of me and the *compañeros*, have to make with the voice all calm, have to chew back on all that crazy shit which makes my balls explode with rage every morning in the reactionary rags, and pushing my head forward like a blow with a mallet, or an infinitely transparent sun, or a bull butting because on the horizon it sees nothing but the red cloth, the whole sky on fire, I have to open my mouth and incant the following words: sure, Skins, that's how we'll fix things, convincingly, definitely, like Napoleon, on and on about the centuries observing us and suchlike crap, and then Alcayaga lets go of my arm and sits down, cleans away a moist bit left over on his cheekbone, gives Mari back her handkerchief, a sopping rag now, and looks out into the street where we're just arriving at the warehouses by Central Station where we'll unload and share out onions, though there are no trucks 'cos the arseholes are on strike and it doesn't matter a toss to them that in the shantytowns there's no rice, no sugar, no pasta, no milk, no flour, no sodding anything, doesn't matter a cuss to them that the old women have to line up at the shops, the cold eating into their tits, withered from so much suckling poor kids, so now we're gonna hand out onions from the kids' own *deux chevaux* and from University buses, and now, looking at Skins who's no longer crying I start to think the same as he thought, and burst out crying too, and Skins sees me and grabs me and says come on now, come on now, don't fuck it up, *compadre.*

the shot's going to come up from low, now the ref's counting out the obligatory number of paces and the wall moves back with a bad grace, always trying to gain an inch here or an inch there, but refs aren't made of cardboard and have their temperaments too so now and again out comes the red card and it's off to watch the match from the touchline, my boy, but now everything's shipshape and the centre-forward comes down kicking up from low, they're grouped there at the entrance to the penalty area and the goalie beats it with his fist and the ball's gonna come down half a pitch from Sportivo Italiano, now Jauregui's got possession, he's taken it on the chest, looking for his team-mates or a tackle from the wing but nobody's marking him. Jauregui still in possession, but now, hold on, yes, he's lobbed it long and deep to Arturo who picks it up at the entrance to the penalty area evades an opponent here comes Rodriguez but he's left on the ground and this means trouble, and the keeper's out of the net and goooaaaaalll, gogogoooaaalll. He took a low deep pass from Jauregui at the entrance to the penalty area, touched it into an arc with the upper edge of his boot as if knocking bricks into place in a wall, danced rings round the defense and went forward to make contact with the leather. In came Rodriguez trying to cut him off with his right, but he feinted from the waist unbalancing him, then when the goalie came out at the last moment he shot under his body making a complete pig's ear of his efforts and goooaaaaaallll gogogooooaaaaaalll to Flecha, Arturo's very own speciality which has brought together several first division scouts out on this remote pitch. Facus, time for the time, and your comments!

twelve minutes into the first half, and as you say a select cluster of soccer technicians have made a date here at this sporting tourney, from where I'm sitting I can make out Dante Pesce, Washington Urrutia and Braulio Musso, so far Arturito has fulfilled all the expectations built up around him this last month and all that remains now is to see if he can keep it up from here on out

that's for sure, Facus, let me tell you I've seen the loveliest footballing roses bloom and wither before the day is out

exactly so, Marquez, it's beholden upon us at all costs to avoid any hint of tropicalistic hyperbole in our commentary or we may sow dreams which nature doesn't allow to bloom

so right, Facus, it's a risky business building glass towers and castles in the air, but it can be said that a move like that holds out hopes of greatness, a young forward with a dizzying waist and commitment, Facus, the courage to dribble right into the penalty area, the guts to risk his knees and a good final touch, because don't ever forget, Facus, that for many inexperienced boys their own moves go to their heads and when they have to deliver the goal it's as if they wake up from a dream and they get stuck outside the goal as if bolted down

very true, Marquez, very true, many look deep frozen when the keeper crosses them, like they've seen a ghost, or a demon, or the bogey-man in person, so they snatch the ball away from them or some beanpole appears ready to grab the birds from the very air or shake hands with the stars, so all the more to Arturo's credit then, Marquez, who, without falling into tropicalism, we can say is potentially a truly valuable discovery

*potentially valuable*, Facus, you've hit the nail on the head there spelling out with the objectivity our listeners merit precisely the moral and sporting stature of young Arturo, a judgement which describes him well, but, and this is im-por-tant, Facus, no commitments

absolutely right, Marquez, and now we're fifteen minutes into the first half, and here comes a commercial break, Facus

score a goal in one: dine out the wife at Santiago Zuñiga's traditional eating house, only yards from the Plaza de Armas, request Santiago's shellfish casserole, rump steak with chipped potatoes, spiced tripe, choose from a vast range of wines and sweets, all accompanied by the traditional cordiality of the house. Or if your preference is pasta, Imola's spaghetti, delicious from tip to tip. Everything for the shoe industry at factory prices at Che Martin's. Visit the Happy Motorist, on the red corner in the bustling 10th of July district. Strike sparks from the road, motor fans, bring your wheels to Lucifer's electrical workshop, open day and night, San Isidro 545, and Flecha are attacking—over to you, Marquez!

effectively so, Facus, a beautiful combination from Jauregui to Arturito out on the far right, and the lad's off like an arrow down the far touchline, Rodriguez's defense collapses, Arturo keeps possession, Tello in to mark him, he stops the ball, bluffs, now the keeper's out to cover the angle, but now Jauregui's alongside and asking for the ball! but Arturo wants to dribble right up to the goalie, jumps over him lifting the ball a little and corner! right at the last moment the keeper saves and puts it into corner—Facus!

well, just as we said, Marquez, the kids come out like new born pups, cling on to the bone, and instead of putting it into the net concentrate on digging their own little hole, because that move of Arturo's, Marquez, was brilliantly worked out

brilliant, Facus

brilliant, Marquez, the move as I was saying finished up in the common grave of the *lapsus linguae*, he went for the nail and flattened his thumb, exactly like a lushly printed book but with an erratum on every page, wouldn't you say, Marquez

exactly as I was going to describe it, Facus, the vocation of the national team's centre-forward at the very mouth of the goal, the masochistic taste for taking in water and sinking just as port is reached after the storm, is endemic, part of the landscape of the country, Facus, built into the chromosomes of the national player, pressed into him like an IBM punch-card that he must lose the move in the penalty area and in this respect we should learn from the Dutch, Facus

how's that, Marquez?

well, as you very well know, not only do they produce great cows with the richest milk, as well as windmills and tulips, they have lately also been exporting players to various European countries

exactly, Marquez, and an illustrative example for our listeners would be the star Johann Cruyff

Croif, Facus

very well, Marquez, Cruif, Croif, Craif, as some others have it, was recently sold to Barcelona for a good fistful of millions

An interesting item of information, Facus, and I'd recommend that with all due haste we despatch a dietician to Holland to observe and rigorously take note of what athletes eat over there, to measure the density of the air and to attend to their modes of entertainment and relaxation in order to reproduce them exactly in our environment

why not, Marquez, why not, just as we arrived at artificial insemination which is after all virtually a challenge to the inscrutable design of the Divinity, so we could achieve the transmutation of the minimum and necessary ecological conditions so that with a similar environment we can produce similar results, so here's hoping our leaders pay attention and don't turn a deaf ear, Marquez

and... I always think you can lead a horse to water, but at the same time God helps those etcetera, and, as Luis Sandrini once said, "electric words, ears unplugged", Facus, and the time now is nineteen minutes into the first half, and here are some words of advice for our listeners: score a goal in one...


"How do you do it?"

Arturo stuck his head out of the water and pushed his ear closer.

"Didn't hear you."

"How d'you do it? How d'you get them all giddy when you go into the penalty area?"

"Inspiration, man. You can't explain it."

"But technique too."

"Technique too."

"Why don't you teach us?"

Arturo covered his head with a towel and began to rub. Jauregui, shivering, climbed into the shower.

"Why should I? One like me in the team is enough. When there's only one, he's worth more. They teach you that crap in school. Didn't you go to school?"

"Primary. Now I work in a leather factory."

"Oh, yeah."

"I like my work!"

The youth set to with his comb, untangling his thick hair and studying Jauregui's ablutions in the mirror.

"Everyone in the city's happy with what they've got. Not me, feller. I want the lot, jumbo-size. You'll never find me in some stinking little factory."

From his bag he extracted a white shirt with a starched collar. Noticing a small globe on the bench, he pushed it with his finger, making it spin on its axis. He did up his buttons and when Jauregui turned off the shower, whirled the sphere again, laughing excitedly. Closing his eyes he stabbed his finger at it, then brought his face down close to it and saw the red stain on the map was Russia.

Jauregui smiled.

"Caught you, man," said Arturo. "You're a commie, that's why you're smiling."

"And what about it?"

"You lot'll end up begging in the streets, bare-arsed and in rags."

"Know what? Seems to me you don't care about the country."

"Sure I care about the country, Jauregui." He picked up the globe and put it near his belly, pressing the blue of its oceans against his penis. "This round little country is what I care about." He began to rotate his hips. "Little darlin'!"

Jauregui stroked his hand down his nose slowly, and watched him, waiting for the jeering expression to spread all over his face.

"Is it a fact you're a virgin?"

From deep inside, the youth felt the coolness of the shower matched by a scarlet current, which rose burning through his body until it reached his eyebrows.

"Who told you that?"

"It's what they say."

"Who?"

"It's what they say, I told you."

Arturo fastened the watch with the elastic strap to his wrist.

"Present from my Grandad."

But the sly look stayed fixed on the other's face, immutable as a mask.

He wound the watch until the screw offered resistance, and looked at himself long and hard in the mirror. He lifted his upper lip and, slightly, his right eyebrow.

"A couple of whores, and we'll sort out this virginity crap tonight," he said to the face in front of him.


The employee they call chief, the ignorant, *maestro*; the waiter, sir; the shoe-shine boy, boss; the assistant, professor; the sick, patient; the male nurse, doctor; the sergeant, captain; the captain, major; the major, general and the simple troopie: corporal.

Lately, Corporal Sepulveda had become a gentle arbiter of the traffic, especially in the mornings, before the routine had worn down the enthusiasm of the spruce shave etched into his cold skin. At the junction of the Costanera and the bridge he lived the irony of restraining and quickening convertibles while he himself hailed from the southern suburbs, a district abundant in handcarts, ancient wagons propelled by flesh and blood, and the remains of 1940s taxis, nurtured by humble district councils. He never felt pride, but alarm certainly, that a uniformed body placed frontally or in profile had the capacity to stop or start again these copious and provocative motors. When the ache in his feet or nostalgia for his evening tipple began to undermine the sharpness of his signal changes, he would mentally add up the thousands of kilometres of passing cars, of the steel chain which grazed against him, tossed him in its slipstream, and fired volleys of flashes at him of chrome-reflected sun, and he would calculate how much these grenades of wind and light were wearing out his pupils. Until finally, like all his colleagues, he had bought a pair of dark glasses, which now blotted out the city with the same muddy tint as that of the river unhurriedly winding its way beneath or beside him.

At this hour in the morning, his signals had the vigour of a gymnast and the politeness of a porter in a classy hotel, serene despite the goading of drivers revving up in neutral to make him unblock the wide mouth of the road leading to the city centre. Years before, it had succeeded in annoying him, this bumptious pedal-pumping, which went unpunished by anything in the traffic regulations, and was as often as not accompanied by a provocative nosing over the white line, invading the pedestrian crossing. To begin with he had censured such annoyances by removing the car to the side of the road, and presenting the driver with a ticket for contempt of authority, an action which only created a jam in the intersection by the bridge which usually ended in bickering and minor accidents which he himself then had to sort out. And then his officer would want to know why he wasn't at his post, and why he had not only allowed a jam to build up but had provoked it by his obsession with handing out fines with the prodigality of a priest pressing images of saints onto old women and children. *Very well, Sepulveda, according to the letter of the law there was an infraction, but on occasions experience, the demands of the moment, a sense of proportion, an intuitive sense of balance, and, above all, the need to avoid a worse evil, oblige us guardians*

74

*of the law to turn a blind eye to venial misdemeanours.*
From then on Sepulveda accustomed himself to
absorb such provocation as mere signs of unbalance
and distress among the drivers who devoured the
Costanera on their way to their banks and businesses
in the centre as if each inch lost was a wholesale
debacle in their cash receipts. Recently, however,
things had got worse, since the folks in the up-market
neighbourhoods of the city went around saying that
the *carabineros* sympathized with the government,
and that the latter was stuffed with people like them,
with their ugly serge uniforms and proletarian lisps.

After a while he had replaced the rule book by a
sharp whistle-blast and a gesture, restrained of hand
but stern of face, demanding that the offending
vehicle move back. This method put the driver in his
place, but also proved inefficient. Some offenders,
livid at having been imprecated by authority—like
vulgar delinquents!—lost all decorum, and in a lather
of fury and impatience, reversed without consulting
their rearview mirrors, catching their bumpers in the
radiators of those behind and leading to jams, insults
and scuffles, when not pathetic dents in the crisp,
dynamic lines of their impeccable machines, as
polished as children washed and brushed by their
mothers and setting off for school. It was enough
that an officer said to him once *Sepulveda, don't
swim against the tide* and *Sepulveda, don't try to
turn back the clock by sticking back the pages on the
calendar* and *Sepulveda, too much dignity is as bad
as too much impudence*, for the corporal to stop using
such measures to censure his clients' anxieties. Years
of practice led him to more subtle and effective meth-
ods: when the arrogant snorts of a Cadillac bore down
on him, or when someone crossed the white line, or
even when the barking horn-blasts came from the

middle of the mass of escaping fumes and throbbing engines, Sepulveda would simply wait longer before giving way, and if he could make out a ponderous and shaky truck crossing the bridge from La Vega market, he would wait until the triumphant wagon was halfway across the Costanera before stepping back a few yards, raising the most dignified of hands, and only then granting permission to move, with the delicious authority of the toreador, cape extended fully on his arm. The effect was easily predictable, as the aggrieved drivers could not resist turning their heads and bestowing upon him a look very similar to spitting at him, as they accelerated on their way. Such procedures might be taken even further by an action which to Sepulveda was the crowning moment of a task impeccably executed: responding to the fist-shaking drivers by tapping two fingers against the peak of his cap.

With time, Sepulveda began to appreciate in himself the marks of maturity, that unarticulated sureness which allowed him to ignore trivialities and carry out his duties with equanimity and relaxed routine. Throughout the past year his body and whistle had been adjusting to the minimum professionally required. Practice showed him that this method, even amidst the morning convulsions on the Costanera, allowed him to dedicate his attention to working out viable alternatives for his plans for his retirement: to become a professional musician.

He had no sentimental problems, having accepted his widowerhood with a fervent sentimentalism that months of mourning had transformed into a precise and sufficient ritual: taking flowers every anniversary.

Lodgings, a problem for so many, were a delight for him. In the *pension* there was no lack of either peace or hubbub, and nobody ever complained about his sessions at the piano. As far as he could perceive the psychology of his fellow lodgers, they needed his playing as much as their dinner in the evenings. Certainly, he got on better with some than with others, but, equally certainly, there was nobody, absolutely nobody, with whom he got on badly. The footballer from the south was a cheeky sort, but he'd never had an angry word from him, and if he were to try it, well, he'd cross that bridge when he came to it: that was most practical.

Suddenly, something out of the ordinary was happening less than a block from his post. Three fast-moving cars were cutting in on another vehicle, pushing it towards the inner pavement, by the river. Somehow, Sepulveda had the sensation that the scene already existed in his mind's eye, experienced by him before, or heard about, or seen in the movies. Taking off his glasses, he saw through the sudden glare that the victim's car had pulled up dead and that another had stopped ahead of it, blocking its way. He saw that very few cars were continuing along the outer lane, and that almost all the traffic had stopped, while the drivers were leaving their vehicles to surround the stationary car and shout at the passenger to get out. When the door opened, a figure in uniform alighted, a general maybe, and Sepulveda, from the vantage point of his wooden dais, saw him confront a tall woman with a masculine hairdo in the centre of the crowd. Stowing his spectacles in his coat, the Corporal began to walk towards the incident. Like a single animal the crowd was already pressing round the uniformed figure, cutting him off increasingly from his car, while two youths knelt down beside the latter's rear wheels. Sepulveda could just see them inserting knives into the valves of

77

the tyres, and hear the hiss of escaping air. As he tried
to clear a way towards the group round the General, he
became aware of his right hand gripping the butt of his
service revolver. Touching it a little lower, he discovered as well that at some moment he had unfastened
the holster. Now, he realized, it was impossible for him
to get any closer, because the crowd had formed a
dense barrier. Nearby the General were two photo-
graphers with their cameras clicking as if it were all a
public show, an ambassadorial visit to the tomb of
some hero. Though nothing in particular had commu-
nicated it to him, the sensation of something desperate invaded Sepulveda's mouth, nothing to do with
the obligatory calm of the agent of public order. It
was as if he'd seen a bird of ill omen crossing a blazing
sky, a vulture with its beak stained with human flesh.
As the sensation became frozen sweat beneath the
green serge of his uniform, he watched himself pushing violently towards the centre of the crowd. A man
was opening the door of a taxi for the General, who
climbed in, and amidst whistles and obscentiies the
vehicle disappeared along the Costanera. In groups
of three, a handful of youths got into four cars,
amongst them the two who had let down the tyres,
and the cars filed away down a sliproad into Provi-
dencia. Sepulveda walked over to the General's car
and motioned with his arm for space to survey the
scene. A middle-aged man, red-faced and thinly blond
at the temples, strutted over to him, his chest thrust
out, while two elegant youths on either side of him
watched Sepulveda gravely.

"Make way!" ordered the Corporal.

The man tensed, and planted himself firmly in
front of him as if turned to stone.

"Where are you off to?" he said to him familiarly.

Sepulveda saw the face of his premonition closing

in, rapidly like a cockroach, dirty like a fly squashed against a windowpane. Now, just as they had encircled the General, they were surrounding him. Around him also they were leaving a circle of asphalt, like saw-dust for a clown, the women tinkling the keys of their cars, the youths fingering short rubber-covered iron bars which had sprouted like lightning from their nails, and all of them with considerable saliva on their lips and a kind of round smile spreading across their mouths like animals.

"Let me through!" ordered Sepulveda, and bent his elbow, gripping his weapon.

The man wrinkled his nose and in concert with the rest released a small sound through his nostrils, a tiny insult, his shoulders hardly shaking, as if scaring off a fly.

"What are you going to do, mother-fucker? Kill a gentleman?"

The Corporal's revolver hand felt weaker than a shadow, while the weapon demanded a firm hand to level its barrel and squeeze and squeeze the trigger. He thought of saying, "You're under arrest," but knew it would be out of proportion, ridiculous, use-less, and he stayed silent with the pistol pointing at the ground and his eyes fixed on its barrel. Once before he had felt like this, when a kid in sixth grade had spat on his fingers and wet his ears with saliva. Only that once had he felt the same, during Aguirre Cerda's government, whose soft indian's face with its friendly moustache had hung in the headmaster's study, and the headmaster had suspended him for a week, for a whole week, and called in his parents, all because the big kid from the sixth had flaked out when he'd kicked him in the balls, had lain there stretched out with his face screwed up in pain, as flat-out as any corpse.

Now, the mannish woman's body under the humiliating sun looked to him like a bird's beak. Clinging to the arm of an adolescent, she had attracted his attention by shaking her car keys very close to his ear. When Sepulveda worked up the strength to look at her, the hard mouth was already open: "Queers!" she said, as if speaking to others as well as him, and drove her keys into his uniform, as if into others as well as him.

That was the day Corporal Sepulveda spent many hours asleep with his eyes open and did not play the piano or come down to dinner.

For minutes nobody had spoken, and the complicity of the silence emphasized the monotonous supping of soup and the mechanical movement of arms. Everything conspired to make matters worse: the breeze whistling through the broken glass and agitating the folds of the tablecloth as in a horror film, the fine decorations covered with dust, and above all the butler, starched stiff, but with a beard like a pirate, who while serving wine to Javier had broken his crystal glass with an incisive blow with the neck of the bottle. The parents conferred upon him an icy glare, and as the flustered butler wrapped up the pieces of glass in his napkin, Javier sat well back in his seat and, opening his eyes and mouth unnaturally wide, simulated the face of a gargoyle. As he covered his mouth with his napkin, Arturo thought that even worse than the guffaw which was fighting to escape would be the little trickle of urine that would almost inevitably follow.

At that precise moment, Señora Marcela wiped away a breadcrumb from the corner of her lip.

"Is your Grandfather still as amorous as ever, Arturito?" Continuing the hare-brained jerking of his neck, and with his cheeks blown out with air, Javier watched his mother and waited triumphantly for his friend to break the silence. Swallowing hard, and with his face criss-crossed by contradictory twitches, Arturo wagged the point of his chin in assent. The woman gave a bored smile: "The older the dog...."

The father knocked his fork against a glass.

"Tender grass for an old bull," he added, with a brief chortle. Surmising that this laugh would have the effect on them of an epidemic, the youths avoided each others' glances, while their fingers wound further into the tablecloth. Arturo closed his eyes, aware that these were the only visible opening through which his guffaw might at any moment explode. The father puffed out his neck and drummed his fork.

"If your grandfather were Minister of Agriculture, he'd have expropriated everything by now, right down to the gardens of this house."

"Including the dirt in your nails," added Señora Marcela.

"Your Grandfather was the greediest old man I ever saw. He wanted to share out everything which didn't belong to him. Even the clover fields, he wanted to expropriate."

"Everything," the lady emphasized.

"Hot as hell with the peasant women, and as political as a priest. Began to talk about expropriations way back in Ibañez's time. You'd have been so high. You used to go down to the pool with Javier to swim every blessed day of the summer. Do you remember how Javierito used to come home on holiday and tell us the jokes from the capital? Do you remember any of those jokes?"

Arturo felt that the limit was approaching, that hardly a muscle or the thinnest membrane was left under control; even if it was a kids' game, he didn't want to lose. He caught a glimpse of Javier, convulsed and contorted, and even believed he could hear the guffaws in his friend's stomach. It was encouraging to see the other was at breaking point, and he smiled at the father.

"And he spent the whole time organising the

peasants into unions." The old man broke a piece of bread. "Until it all worked out for them."

"Until it worked out," chorused the woman, arranging her hair against her ear.

"It took a while, but finally it worked. Now they must have a piggery in the chapel, eh, Arturo?"

The youth had to open his mouth wide to take in air.

"My God!" said the mother. "He's choking, the poor thing."

"A co..." cried Arturo, red and perspiring, coughing, laughing, swallowing air, wiping his eyes with the back of his hand.

"A what?" she said.

"A cooperative." Swallowing the contents of his nose, he found he could speak. "They set up a cooperative in the church!"

Javier tore round the table and grabbing him by the neck pushed him to the ground, and sat on him, tickling him everywhere Arturo's hands let him.

"Javier!" said his mother.

"Open your mouth and the flies get in!" whooped her son, thrusting his fingers into the other's stomach and revolving them, until Arturo cried out, stifled by laughter, "Sorry, sorry, please," and still laughing and weeping, and trying to lift his head, he managed to look up at the lady and say: "Beg your pardon, Señora Marcela."


They abandoned the little garden table with its flies luxuriating in the sugar and coffee dregs. the old man gripped a walking stick, which he didn't need, and walked away leaning on it like a tripper in a rotting jungle, a decay of weeds and small animals. From his aristocratic nose hung a mixture of anguish and disdain.

"Weeds!" he said, thrusting his stick into the moss. "There used to be gladioli here, and this was a walnut tree. But the weeds and dust come quickly." He put an arm round Arturo's shoulders and invited him to walk with him. "It takes a century to achieve the loveliest roses, and only a few months for the weeds to stifle everything. They were waiting underground. Like death. But they weren't dead. They were like a worm eating the roots of the flowers, faster than a hare; d'you follow me, Arturo?" The boy nodded, distracted by the breasts of a Diana the Hunter who crowned a fountain of muddy water. "Like her, do you?"

"Yes, sir."

"Look carefully at that young woman. How much do you think she cost me?"

"No idea, sir."

"Exactly thirty. And anywhere in the world they'd give me three times as much."

"Why don't you sell it in the United States, then?"

The man tore up a handful of weeds which were covering his feet, and threw them far away as if they were a hot mass of dung.

"Why not? Because I haven't. I'm going to leave her here for the birds to peck at and the worms to drool over. Understand?"

"Yes sir."

"Do you have any coins?" Arturo took one and made it dance in his fist as if preparing to throw a die. "Dead fish! Give one to Javier, and take another for yourself."

The youths held their arms forward, and at the word from the old man tossed the coins, hearing their splashes in the scummy water.

"What did you wish for?"

Javier shrugged. "Money," he said.

"Arturito?"

"Women."

Then the old man threw his coin with a despairing wrist and his eyes focussed way beyond the water.

"What was it, papa?"

"A miracle, Javierito."

Supported on his stick, he wheeled round and walked away towards the house. With his back to them, he said:

"I think I'll go and get myself a drink."


His friend held him back with a tug at his sleeve. His hands were held in the air and with a knowing gesture he watched the old man retreat. Then he pointed towards the cabin, and with a wink asked Arturo to follow. Producing a rusty bunch of keys, he fiddled with the thickest until the latch gave way. After switching on the light, he turned his head to enjoy Arturo's surprise. There were heaps of paintings, mostly landscapes, sets of crystalware on a desk, dusty bottles of wine piled in boxes, woven filigree carpets, useless bundles.

"How about this, then?"

"What's it all for?"

"To get out, to sell up." Javier went over to one of the boxes and, taking a corkscrew from his trouser pocket, unstopped the first bottle. He rubbed the label and proudly showed off the year and the vineyard. Arturo took hold of the neck of the bottle and drank a measure somewhat larger than his friend's. "This was the gardener's hut."

At the second swig, the bottle was almost empty.

"Listen, Javier," said Arturo, grabbing him as if frantically inspired. "D'you know any birds?"

His friend despatched the remaining liquid, and

with sudden discomfort extricated himself from the hands which gripped his shoulders.

"That gardener was worse than your Grandad with the women. D'you ever read that novel about the gardener who had it off with the lady of the house?"

"Lady Chatterley's Lover?"

"Well, this guy was the same. He had the lady of this house."

"Your mother?"

"Exactly."

"Don't be filthy." Arturo glanced sideways at the box containing the bottles. "You sure?"

"It's true."

Javier took out two delicately engraved crystal goblets and passed his finger-tips over them as if caressing some excitingly stimulating skin. He filled them from the second bottle, dark as thick blood.

"Mother says this crystal is as sacred as a chalice." Poking out his tongue, and with his eyes half-closed, he licked the rim.

They drank with their heads thrown back until their nostrils were parallel with the roof.

"Copy me," said Javier, and, without looking at the wall, smashed the goblet against the rustic wood. Arturo watched the fragments shatter with a musical sweetness. He balanced the goblet, extended his toe as if bowling, and loosed off the crystal gently. The fragments were less fine, but the music incomparably purer. Javier took up a new glass, this time between two fingers, and invited Arturo to do the same.

"One for each chick brought here by the gardener!"

"Your mother'll kill you!"

Javier aimed at the door-knob and released the crystal, scoring a bullseye.

"For all the maids brought here by our fine gardener! For my mother's friends brought here by our stupendous gardener!" He struck out at the goblet held in Arturo's hand, but before reaching it stopped short, smiling. Replacing it delicately with the rest of the service, he picked up the jug instead, by its base. All around the room its brilliance reflected the colours of the tapestries hanging on the walls. "For mother, fuckface!" And he let it fall, pulverized, at his feet.

Arturo swallowed. He was almost certain that Doña Marcela had heard the last explosion from the house.

"That's enough. Let's go and look for women!"

Javier drank from the bottle, and shuddered theatrically with pleasure.

"I'm going to show you something you'll like much more. Block the door with that sofa."

The youth hesitated, so Javier shoved the sofa over roughly. Then he knelt down and carefully inserted the corkscrew into an almost imperceptible slit in the plush. Pushing with his fingers, he lifted a patch, revealing a space big enough for both his hands to fit. Before removing them again, he bit his tongue and with his eyes indicated to Arturo that he should kneel down too. He was showing him a pistol. He raised his hands and breathed on the metal as if reviving a wounded bird. When Arturo looked at his friend's eyes, they were calm, sweet.

"Like it?"

"Is it loaded?"

"Don't be afraid."

He put his arm back into the hold and with enormous gentleness drew out onto the carpet a short-barrelled submachine gun and then, immediately afterwards, a little box covered with the same material as the sofa. When he opened it, the bullets, arranged like gold teeth, reflected the light falling on them vertically from the bulb. He drummed his fingers on them as if playing a tune on a xylophone.

"What have you got these here for? Why all the guns?"

Javier tightened his lips brusquely.

"Last year Papa got an urge to play cowboys. But that game's over now."

"What do you mean?"

"Seems it's time for the boys who really know their stuff to take over."

"I don't understand."

"No news from the front, Lieutenant Arturo?" He gripped the pistol, then let it go to lay it in the palms of his friend's hands. "Stick it under your jacket. It's a present."

"Are you crazy?"

"It's a present, idiot. No discussion."

Arturo felt the inside pocket of his jacket, and put the gun inside. He fastened the button of the pocket, as gently as a careful mother.

He touched the weapon through the cloth, where it lay awkwardly, like fear. Then he wiped the hand he had touched it with on his thigh, as if he had committed a crime and instead of wiping away his fingerprints wanted absurdly to wipe out the murderous hand itself. Javier put a handful of bullets in his friend's pocket, and rattled them complicitously with a couple of light taps. Then he lifted the same hand to the back of his neck, and stroked the ends of his lank hair.

"Seriously, Javier, don't you know any chicks?"

His friend savoured the final drops from the second bottle, then rolled it on the carpet, as if ironing it.

"Chicks," he said. "Okay, then. We'll go in the car."

"Magic! Hey, Javier, I want to leave the bullets here."

"What bullets, fuckface?" He leant on Arturo's shoulder. Then his attempts to replace the sofa sent him onto his back, where he lay with his legs at right angles to the roof. Hanging on to Arturo's arm, he began to lift himself off the floor, but on the point of regaining his balance hurled himself backwards, pulling his friend down with him. A layer of dust stirred, hung in the thick air, and made them cough.

"This muck is the clouds and we're in heaven. Let's stay here, fuckface."

"I want to go out."

"If you want to go out, then out we go."

He walked reeling over to the sofa, but instead of trying to move it collapsed onto it. Arturo took over; once outside, Javier grabbed him round the waist, and lifted him, making them stumble several times before reaching the car.

"Fly, fuckface! Fly me to the moon! Miami! Dog tracks. Velvet suits. The Sinatra clan. The Braniff family, buddy."

Arturo watched the other's third failed attempt to insert the key into the ignition. He couldn't decide whether to get out, start the ignition himself, or start on the third bottle.

"Something wrong?" said Javier.

"Nope."

"Right, then. Magic, then."

Emerging from the doorway, Javier's father greeted them, a bottle of whisky in one hand and a glass in the other. He put down the bottle for a second to wave away the car fumes that surrounded him, then, supporting himself on one knee, raised his elbow to serve himself another dose.

He liked this politician because he was everything he was not: tall as a lily or a candle in the church, with large eyes and spiritual hands like invisible doves. He liked it too that he was his secretary, at the same time as being the only other inhabitant of the court. From his wicker throne, crowned with *copihue* flowers, he said, "We'll solve the meat shortage—by eating the rabbits. Go and tell them to slaughter them!" "The rabbits have gone, señor," said the gentle politician. "So what's your advice?" "That we should transfer to the beaches. There we just need worms for bait, a line and a steel hook, and we'll have all the fish we need." "And what of the kingdom?" "We are the kingdom. Wherever we are, there it is." "Given the small number of inhabitants we are, your argument is perfect. We're a small country, but quick." "Well said, your majesty. As long as no disagreements arise between us everything will be fine. And even if we should quarrel, hey ho and each to his home, and that's the end of the story." "One man alone is not a country, secretary. You need at least two." The man, thin as a saint, placed a finger to his forehead. "It seems to me, your majesty, that you are not well. You have a fever once again." "No problem," said Señor Pequeño. "Birds are my favourite creatures, and they sing all day because their bodies are warmer than those of other animals, and more than a country or a person, I'd like to be a bird." "I don't understand symbols, sire. I am no more than a confidante, a discreet secretary and amateur hunter. I must insist that if we have no rabbits—because there are none, or because they hide them from us—we must take the healthiest way out: climb the highest mountain and nourish ourselves on birds of prey and deer." "You decide, secretary, what we should do and how we should dress for it." "Grey for the mountains, with white jerkins for when it snows. If we go to the beach, on the other hand, to catch fish, I recommend blue suits and a cartload of lemons to dress the dinner." Señor Pequeño alighted from his throne, placed the *copihues* around his waist like a scimitar of shining petals, and made off towards the ocean with the chair on his back, while the refined politician loaded a portion of lemons into the wicker basket, and although their progress through the hills, under a sweetly cloudy sky, was slow, they always found themselves at a point from which the whole world, empty of people, could be seen. Each step brought them closer to the sea, but also to the mountains, to Argentina, Poland, Australia, Iceland and England. "Doesn't it seem strange to you?" asked Señor Pequeño. "It doesn't seem strange to me, because I believe we're dead. But don't be concerned, Señor Pequeño, because we are also death."

Señor Pequeño became aware of the danger when his ears pricked up. Over the edge of the newspaper which aided his sleep, a red-haired man was approaching followed by a kind of twin, only slightly taller and sporting fashionable heels, like a dude. With transparent certainty it came to the little man that dealings with these individuals would not be to his benefit. Lamenting the interruption of his trip with the gentle politician with magic hands, he began to edge the newspaper discreetly upwards, with the firm intention of hiding himself and as far as possible beginning again at the moment where the secretary said: "We also are death".

All the subtlety of his movement disappeared at a stroke when the shorter redhead jutted out a vigorous finger, which drew behind it a tense and horizontal arm, the finger and the arm together pointing directly at Señor Pequeño's heart, while the larger redhead aimed at his forehead, but this time not with a finger but with a weapon whose flashing in the sunlight blinded him. As he began his flight, as if in a matinee at the local movie house, but making tracks on his very own quite tiny feet, it occurred to Señor Pequeño that reality has a certain flavour of truth, a certain grief, lacking in dreams. As his heart pattered, it also crossed his mind that he would have preferred this persecution to have been a dream and his country to be translated into precise reality. As he turned the corner, the first sweat appeared on his eyelids and that sticky sensation, corrosive of his sartorial neatness, came over his neck. In the time it took to feel this, he ran the length of the block. Keeping up his pace, he turned the next corner, where he stopped for three seconds, enough to take in three substantial mouthfuls of air and locate the redheads, who were swallowing the yards, but as awkwardly as asthmatics. He felt like a fox as he took off again, as cunning as the puppet fox which gobbled up the puppet pigs in his show. Turning the last corner, in seconds he was breathing in urgently needed oxygen, under the same sentimental telegraph pole where he had dreamt his exile. Somewhat slower now, he reached the corner, folded the newspaper, and gestured with it to stop a bus. From the doorway as he boarded the bus he could see the redheads running towards him, finger and pistol aloft, and simultaneously he saw the Beast erupt like a hammerblow from the secret door of the cockpit, his huge somnambulant head looking towards the panting redheads, who diverted their finger and pistol towards the door of the pit, or rather at the Beast's chest, at which he began to run, driven on by the flapping of the cock and punishing the paving stones like a steam locomotive, presumably heading for the bus. Señor Pequeño received his ticket and said to the driver, "Get this thing moving, señor. It's a matter of life and death!"

As the man simply stared at him with an expression somewhere between fear and irony, he raised two fingers held stiffly inside his jacket pocket and pointed at his temple. Deducing there was something alarming inside, the driver immediately brought his foot down hard on the accelerator.

"You're very understanding," said Señor Pequeño, and went to sit down at the far end of the bus.


After it seemed to him that he had left the bus, and had walked half a block, the policeman called him over with two fingers, making a kind of brushing motion in the air. Ever respectful of the law, Señor Lecaros obeyed.

"Where are you off to?" asked the man in green.

Señor Pequeño thought it prudent to indicate with a finger the direction he had just come from.

"That's not a place. People go to some particular place."

"Over there."

"Where?" Señor Pequeño rocked on his heels, a doubtful expression playing about his mouth, meditating on the cardinal features of the situation. One last time he raised his finger and pointed in the same direction. He was convinced that things were going well, and that so far he had not fallen into any contradictions. "That's not a place, I said. I'm asking you to give me the name of some street, or neighbourhood.

Didn't you know that neighbourhoods have names? Ah, never mind. Got a light?"

"Yes. Here you are."

"Smoke?"

"Yes."

"Do you have a ciggy?" The little man offered a pack of standard Cabañas. The policeman took one, and put it behind his ear, close to his temple. Suddenly, the constable became involved in a lengthy and involved contest between his hands, his belt and his trousers, which tended to fall down. He finished the manoeuvre by tightening his fly-zip until he had difficulty breathing, He was left with his chest pushed out, which made his voice sound somewhat forced. "Well, as far as you're concerned, it'd be best for you to come along to the station. There are a lot of odd customers around loose, and who knows what might become of you." A malevolent smile revealed a gold tooth. Simultaneously, his back pocket slid gradually down his behind. From it he extracted a folded piece of paper, which, when spread out in the bright light of midday, revealed itself to be a black-and-white photograph, but with some details touched up in colour: red cheeks and lilac spectacles. "How many of these people do you know? One... two... three?"

Señor Pequeño tilted his head, feeling how his hand sought to glide over the texture of the image as if the bodies were warm. The figures were those of his father, mother and himself as a child. It was no snap taken in a square or by a threepenny pavement photographer. The three were posing before a backdrop painted with the Eiffel Tower, bohemian French types, berets, mousey moustaches and women in fishnet stockings.

"See? It's best we go to the station."

"Am I under arrest?"

They began walking, close together, while the policeman fanned himself with the photo in the hot and sterile air of the Gran Avenida. An apple seller walked in front of them, swallowed by his apron. The policeman stopped and selected two fat fruit from his basket. He rubbed them on the serge of his uniform until they glowed. He handed one to Señor Pequeño, and they walked on munching them.

"What are we going to do with you, Señor Lecaros?" said the station Commissioner, scratching the point of his chin. Under his elbow was an abundant heap of casesheets. "I ask you, what would you do in my place?" Running his finger under the lines, he read, "1966, theft of savings from a grocer's widow. A grocer's widow, I ask you! And here: re-sale of tickets for the University Classic at the National Stadium! Really, Señor! Can it be that at your age you're still up to the same tricks? Leave it to the rich—they have the edge in this kind of thing. And what's all this? 1970, immoral acts at the Hellfire Club. What was that then? What were you doing that was immoral? Not a striptease, I suppose."

"Is that what it says there?"

"You don't believe the sheet?"

"I have always been extremely proper. My acts have been seen in convent schools."

"Did you or did you not perform in the Hellfire Club in 1968? September 18, 1968."

"What year is it now?"

The Commissioner consulted the calendar.

"1973, now."

"Was it long ago?"

"Five years."

"I don't remember."

"Drunk and disorderly in the Polish ambassador's car. Do you remember that?"

"What year?"

"1965."

"The car I don't remember, Señor Commissioner. D'you have it all there on the paper?"

An elegantly dressed man could no longer put up with being sat on the bench with the other detainees, and approached the desk, face to face with the Commissioner.

"Excuse me, Señor," he said, "but I've been here for an hour waiting to make a statement."

The Commissioner smoothed the recalcitrant corner of a casesheet with his palm.

"The faster we go, the quicker we'll get to you."

"I just wanted to explain..."

"...and as we finish with one, so we start on another."

"I'm very sorry. But I have my documents here. My professional qualifications."

The policeman stood up and, greeting the other detainees, held up the casesheet.

"Begging your pardons, señores; but we're just going to spend a minute looking at these photos."

The group of men and women smiled their assent hastily.

The Commissioner invited Señor Pequeño to sit at his desk, and shone the lamp on the casesheet.

"I want you to put yourself mentally and physically in my place, Señor Lecaros. Read your casesheet Study the photographs, think about them, then tell me with your hand on your heart what I should do with you." He waited until the little man was facing his *curriculum vitae* and, as soon as he was absorbed in it, swept his gaze across the facing groups. "Who's next?" he shouted.

The young woman put out her muscular legs, clad in laddered stockings, over which was spread an imitation leather mini-skirt. Her voluminous breasts perspired beneath a semi-transparent blouse under which could be seen a rose-coloured bra.

"Me, Commissioner," she said, smiling like a schoolgirl.

The policeman kicked the spitoon, crashing it against the wall. He breathed in deeply, and then out again, his face held in his twitching fingers, until he seemed himself again, as if recently emerged from a thermal bath.

"Don't tell me things went wrong with the job! Despite my advice?"

The young woman had wound up the strap of her shoulder-bag, and released it, making it spin round like a top.

"It's not that, Commissioner. I just couldn't get used to the factory."

"So you prefer walking the streets at night! Working with that pretty thing where your belly ends! Am I right?"

"It's not that, Commissioner."

The officer took them all in with a single sweeping gesture.

"None of you like work, that's your problem." The prisoners lowered their heads and only caught the furious boots pacing from one side of the room to the other. "You make me nervous," he said, chewing his words. "Take a seat, my child." He went over to Señor Pequeño and slammed the file shut in his face. "Now what do you have to say? Refreshed your memory?"

The little man raised his hand to this throat to arrange the knot of his tie, but couldn't find it.

"What do you have to say now? Answer me!"

"I don't know what to answer you."

"Oh, perfect! That's a good reply. And now what am I supposed to do with you, answer me that. Threatening a bus driver with two fingers in your jacket pocket! How... where the hell do you get these ideas?"

"Inspiration, Señor Commissioner."

The officer closed the file once again, indicated to Señor Pequeño that he should get up, and sank down into the rotating chair.

"What do I do with you now? What's your advice?"

Señor Pequeño looked timidly towards the door, and then tentatively upwards until his eyes almost met the officer's.

"That you let me go."

The Commissioner nodded gravely, and clapped his hands together.

"Guard!" he shouted. "This one's leaving!"

For a while now the ray of light had shone through the slowly turning dust, spilling over the pillow and wall. Slowly it crept up his jaw, until it reached his nose, at which his eyelashes reacted and his hand reached up to cover his face. With the five fingers extended and held up high, he turned his trunk uncomfortably to the left. Which was when he came across the shoulder straps of the rose-coloured petticoat buried warmly in the dark back; and above them the woman's black hair falling around her with the same placidness as her sleep. The youth wanted to wet his lips, but his saliva was still scorching and thick with alcohol, like the secretions of a cold mixed with sundry tipples. He felt clandestine in that room, suspicious between such elegant walls, with their English hunting prints, complete with hounds, foxes, golden trumpets, and geezers sitting erect in riding hats, red dress jackets and white breeches. Unaware of his own movements, he lowered his hand, turned his cheeks towards the sun, and with his fingertips took hold of the sheet which reached up to the woman's dusky waist and turned it down to her knees. The ample legs were held tightly in brief panties, almost submerged in the folds of her elastic flesh. Trying not to breathe, he gazed his fill at the upper part of her buttock, then lay calmly, biting his nails. Finally, he made up his mind, fully aware of the risks of the manoeuvre. Anchoring his left shoulder on the mattress, he raised his trunk on it until his neck reached over the woman's back and he could peep at her face and breasts. He returned to his post worn out by the effort of his indiscretion and had to breathe deeply. "Holy shit!" he said, very quietly. "She ain't half bad, the little fool." A glance to his right revealed blood on the pillow. He put his hand to his cheek, and it came away with a red stain on the fingers. "One of two things," he thought, as he walked over to the mirror. "Either they kicked the hell out of me, or this *negra* began her career last night." He had to glue his nose to the glass to make out his cheek, split and spattered with blood. "They kicked the hell out of me," he said to himself as his knees almost buckled under him, the victims of a sudden giddiness. He turned his profile to the mirror to contemplate his long hair. "At least they didn't make with the scissors." He approached the bed from the right hand side and, kneeling beside the woman, enjoyed for a few seconds the breath from her broad mouth, half-open as if ready to be kissed.

"Negra," he said, burying his fingers in her shoulder, "they knocked me all to hell."

The woman opened her eyes like a groggy boxer, closed them again, then opened and closed them once more, before pressing her fingers against the bridge of her nose as if switching an electric current on and off, and looking Arturo directly and definitely in the eye. The youth reckoned her at thirty or so.

"They beat me all to hell, Negra," he said, pulling on the elastic of his briefs.

"Sure, I know."

"Fixed me up proper, see." He twisted his neck to the right for her to appreciate the damage. "Look at this."

The woman sighed, arranging a wayward lock of hair behind her ear.

"Not again."

"Eh?"

"The same thing all night long, fat boy. Feel me here, feel me there, they knocked the shit out of me. So, they knocked the shit out of you, and that's that. Now belt up about it."

Arturo pinched his lip and blinked repeatedly with his eyes fixed on the woman's mouth, turning over what she had said. "Fat boy," she'd said. "This chick's round the bend," he thought. "She could call me anything she likes. But 'Fat boy', me! Never!"

"Didn't you see the cut by the eye?"

"Sure. They also knocked the shit out of your eye."

After a yawn she couldn't hold back, the woman slowly closed her eyes. The youth followed her breathing as it settled slowly into calm. For more than a minute he hesitated, winding the corner of the sheet around his thumb. When he had made up his mind, he put his mouth very close to her ear, and tried out a humble smile, more hopeful than gentle.

"Negra, how was I?" he said, with a voice as confidential as her breathing.

The woman didn't open her eyes. "What?"

"In bed, Negra. How was my performance?"

"Why d'you want to know that?"

"Just do."

"What's it matter to you?"

"It does, that's all."

The woman located the same lock of rebellious hair behind her ear, and flattened it down with the palm of her hand. Her nails were green, and there was a copper ring with a reddish stone on her fourth finger.

"You really want to know?"

She opened her eyes fully, and for the first time the young man saw her coffee-coloured eyes, which immediately began to spark mockingly. Their expressions grew different, his ever softer, like a beggar

101

full of tales, and hers tightening, ever more surly as it awoke for the day's first act of survival.

Arturo tried to force the issue.

"Average?"

"Are you seriously asking?"

"Worse than average?"

"Worse. Worse than average, fat boy."

He swallowed.

"Bloody 'orrible?"

"Worse, kid. Not a dicky bird. Gettit?"

"Not a dicky bird? What do you mean, not a dicky bird?"

He threw himself from the bedspread, and tore it off her, as if displaying her triumphantly, all petticoat and breasts, hair tousled and hips warm. The woman drew back, plunging her body down into her thighs. Arturo was on his feet, and trembling with the need to grab something.

The woman jerked away to the other side of the bed.

"Nothing, fat boy, not a damn thing. You went to sleep, gettit?"

At that, the youth went over to the curtains and tugged at the cord, letting in the sun and draught like bullets. The sudden brilliance burst upon the woman, making her cross her forearms in front of her face.

"Shut them, for fuck's sake!" she screamed.

"Don't like the light 'cos it shows up your wrinkles, eh? Makes you look old and shagged out, ain't that right?"

"Shut them, I said."

Back at the mirror, he stretched his eyelid until the violet patch spread painfully.

"Fixed me up proper," he murmured. "How many did it take, Negra?"

She had put on her shoes and was now wrapping herself in a tartan skirt like those used at school.

"How many what?"

"To work me over."

"Just one, sucker."

"A big guy, was he?"

"About so big, creep." She indicated something about the size of a pin.

His fist in his mouth, he chewed at the knuckles until the woman was completely dressed.

"You owe me, fat boy. That'll be three hundred."

"Oh, no. I've got no money."

"Nothing to do with me. You have to pay up."

"What am I supposed to do?"

"A deal's a deal, sucker. Out with it!"

"I told you, I don't have a penny." He went over to the mirror, and in three movements knotted his tie. The woman stood behind him, swinging her bag. "And if I don't pay up, what'll you do about it?" he said, peering at her in the mirror.

"All I can say is it wouldn't be healthy."

"Oh really! Some pimp'll be up to sort me out, is that it?"

"Something like that."

The youth turned round and displayed a pair of empty palms.

"I'm very sorry, Negrita, but I don't have any money, God's truth."

The woman pointed at his wrist.

"The watch."

"A quarter past eleven."

"Not the time, stupid. Give it here."

"Are you crazy? It's a present from my Grandad."

"Hand it over!"

The woman gripped his arm and with the other hand pulled at the elastic strap. The young man twisted his fist round, and covered it with his hand. For several seconds they tussled. She loosened her grip, only to bury her nails in the back of his hand. Three drips of blood trickled down to his knuckles. Arturo evaluated the injuries, as if playing a round of cards. Then he undid the strap, and placed the watch in the *negra*'s palm.

"Thanks, fat boy."


When Arturo saw Señor Pequeño standing on the corner reading the letter, he had the impression that black cats were suddenly multiplying in his path. As he drew closer to the unavoidable spot occupied by the little man in the funereal black suit, he wished he had lived in the era of discovery, so he could have been the king of an island organised as he liked, with his favourite people, docile women, and without shadows or animals of ill omen. When he passed Señor Pequeño at an accelerating pace, the latter drew up beside him, waving the letter above his shoulder. Only after they had walked half a block, with Arturo pretending he had not seen him, did Señor Pequeño speak.

"Good morning."

"Morning," said Arturo, without looking at him or stopping.

"Something the matter?"

"What do you mean?"

"You seem worried." He saw the little man touch his eyes and cheekbones to explain what he meant by "worried". Arturo did not make a habit of spitting, either in the street or on the field, but this time he did, against the wall. "I only ask," admitted Señor Pequeño, "because I do have a problem. And it occurred to me that you might have one too."

"I don't tell no one my problems or my dreams."

"I need money. I've received a letter from certain

gents who, if I don't pay off a certain debt, are going to kill me."

Arturo took the paper from him and read it as they reached the doorway of the *pension*. He put it back in the other's fist as if throwing it into the waste bin.

"You're in the shit," he said. "Where are you going to get the dough?"

"Can you lend it to me?"

"No. Sorry."

He entered the passageway yawning, which brought the collection of pains back to his face. All of a sudden, with a clean 180-degree turn, he was back beside Señor Pequeño within three steps, plunging his arm into his jacket and putting the revolver into his hand.

"Take this. Defend yourself."

Señor Pequeño stepped back, and the weight of the weapon pulled his arm towards the ground. In that moment of suspense, he looked at Arturo like a dog. The youth put a handful of ammunition in the upper pocket of his jacket, where Señor Pequeño sported a dubious handkerchief.

"Keep it, man. You're going to need it."

The little man put the weapon in his pocket, while Arturo yawned over his sleek and oily hair with sudden laziness, but summoning all his strength to limit the painful widening of his mouth. The little man waited patiently for the performance to finish and tapped his jacket pocket.

"You put the bullets inside."

"And what do I do with it then?"

"If they attack you, you shoot. Got it?"

He turned his back on the little man as if suffering another spectacular yawn, and added:

"You can commit suicide with it too, if you want."

Several more minutes passed in which the little

man suspended all thought and was at the point of closing his eyes and returning to his exodus with the gentlemanly politician; but the void in his mind was so complete that he stayed transfixed in the street like an advertising billboard.

"Father! Father!"

The Beast was approaching, blotting out the sun with his immense frame, his blue eyes traced with red veins as if advertising the wine he had consumed. Stinting neither stench nor passion, he grabbed Señor Pequeño and lifted him up to embrace him. The little man delivered several ineffective kicks in the region of the other's thighs.

"What did you say?"

The Beast held him away from him for a second. For the first time Señor Pequeño was as tall as the big fellow, and could not escape a feeling of shock at the pristine grey of his partner's eyes: "Sailor's son", he decided.

"Father," said the Beast. "You're my father!" and smiled from ear to ear, his white teeth as present and correct as cubes of ice.

"Put me down!" ordered Señor Pequeño, delivering a last kick a little above the thigh. "It's utterly idiotic for you to call me father. My hips fit into one of your hands, as you have just demonstrated. Don't you find it ridiculous that I should be the father of a great ape like you?"

"There are tall children with small parents."

"Furthermore, I faint when you lift me up. Stupid sensations come over me, poetic emotions. I felt like a leaf on a tree. We can't have that, do you understand?" The Beast could not make out that his partner was burning up with embarrassment, largely because Señor Pequeño's face was always as palid as a mime artist's. He himself couldn't remember ever having seen blood. What's more, the very idea that he could have such red matter within his own flesh gave him the beginnings of nausea. "You can't go around grabbing people and lifting them up in such an exaggerated way! Do you understand?"

"Yes, Father."

"Very well, then. It's just as well you've arrived because we're in difficulties." He lifted his eyes a couple of feet and bestowed upon him the most intense of his diagonal looks. With the edge of his hand, he gestured as if his throat were being cut. "Serious difficulties." He kept up the look. "I don't suppose you have any money." The Beast agreed fervently. "I didn't imagine so. It's no mystery for anyone that you don't have any money."

"I do what I can, Dad."

"I'm not reproaching you. But the fact is, we need money." He gestured for them both to go and sit on the curb. "Tell me how things went with the bird," he said with a confidential tone of voice and look.

"There are fights on Sundays. We can take the chicken and bet all we like."

"Perfect." He put a hand in his pocket, to pull out only three notes and some coins. "This change is all I've got. Sunday mornings, you said?" The Beast agreed with a huge nod of his head. "How's the chicken?"

"Affectionate as ever."

"Perfect. It's not long 'til Sunday and there's nothing to be gained from confusing things. You can go along on Sunday and bet a lot, but without taking along any money. Then when our chicken kills the others you get the others' money and we'll be rich."

"In other words, I trick them."

"Don't talk so much and cheer up because I'm now going to take you for a glass of wine."

He stood up and patted his behind meticulously until there was not a particle of dust to be seen on the shining cloth. The Beast's tongue felt dry, but after dampening it in the air, as if the latter were an aperitif, he kept control of it all the way to the bar. But by then impatience made impertinence get the better of him.

"Where have you been the past few days, Dad? What were you up to?"

Señor Pequeño released a small quantity of wind, which, compressed by the narrowness of his oesophagus, produced a disproportionately full sound.

"I don't remember," he said, leaning his elbows on the bar.

through the mist you can see them coming puffing like toy trains, and you imagine their icy noses, the wind soaking their clothes, like trees in the morning, and the cold enough to kill you, as if in this damn neighbourhood the *cordillera* itself was plotting against us—that'd be rich, Negro, the *cordillera* itself out to get us!—and I peer out of the window of the hut and have to wipe the glass and afterwards put my hand on the stove because it's frozen up like a cold cut, and they keep coming, the *compañeros*, with their throats clasped in scarves, they keep coming, the buggers, the whole way on foot 'cos it's five days now since the buses joined the strike, and between the bus owners and the lorry owners and the shop-owners they reckon they've got us plucked and stuffed, but look how these folks arrive on foot at the factory! they'd shit themselves if they could see their noses all frozen and the *compañeros* put on their overalls and you ask them, "far to walk, *compañero* Espinoza?" and the bugger lives in Tropezon, get it Mari? in *Tropezon*, but he replies: a fair way, and I want to burst my fat and rounded balls when they come out with that; and Berta Santelices, who lives in La Cisterna: any trouble getting here, *compañera*? and she replies: a bit; and I swear to you Negro, I should be a composer of tangos, these folks are invincible, Negrito, they're made of iron, when I remember the faces on them as they arrive as I'm doing guard rota in the hut I think what did we do to deserve such incredible people, and then El Negro doesn't get me, takes all the colour out of it, Mari, and starts on about Recabarren and Elias Lafferte and Santa Maria de Iquique and the clandestinity of the party under Gonzalez Videla, the Bible in authorized and revised versions, kid; and me, hold on Negro, all I'm saying is that these buggers are like trees, or the wind, or houses, Negro, I'm not asking for the whole glorious history of the never-sufficiently-praiseable Party, I'm just saying what I feel, that's all; and El Negro, who's the first to go to the kiosk to buy the Party paper, to keep up the finances of the Party paper, to talk to the *compañero* newsboy who also belongs to the Party, says to me, most probably with his hand on his Party card: I understand, Fats, you're a sentimental lad and you like to communicate your emotions, and that's fine, but not me, Fats, I want to know the why and wherefore of things, and where they come from and where they lead to, and all this that gets you so worked up is called proletarian class consciousness and it's your duty to know it; so right there, Mari, I have to get down on my knees before him and beg him by all the saints, don't go on, don't go on, I understand all that, and El Negro, why do you ask me, then, for pity's sake, Negro, I told you I didn't ask you anything, fine, then, why do you say these things when I'm around, 'cos you know a serious militant has to explain these things when a *compañero* has doubts; but Negrito, for the love of God and the Most Holy Virgin, I say, I don't have any doubts, not a single one, not the smallest one, not even one this size, and I show him the smallest nail on my thinnest finger, not even a bit of a doubt like this, Negrito, and El Negro: I just thought, and that's where we were when the boys from the Security Committee turned up exactly twenty minutes before the beginning of the first shift, and say *compañero* Osorio, we're meeting here urgently because a problem has come up, and I look at El Negro and say, fine, *compañeros*, I'll leave you to it, then, but then it's El Negro who gets up and carefully folds his paper on the table and says to me, I personally asked for you to be put in charge of this case; but, Negro, says I, I'm just rank and file around here, how am I going to get mixed up in security; and El Negro says, you have to get involved, or a *compañero* in the factory is in for a rough time; which is when the Security Delegate says, that's enough, Negro, belt up, Negro, that's just what mustn't happen, putting prejudices into the *compañero*'s mind, and El Negro, sure, you're right, *compañeros*, and off he goes, and so there we are, Mari, your poor old Fats has to take charge of the whole mess: *compañero* Osorio, do you know *compañero* Oliva, sure I know him, what's up with him, well, we have a problem with him which affects the running of this state sector factory, what are you on about, why are you looking so serious, well, *compañero*, calling a spade a spade, Oliva has been selling his monthly quota of cloth from the factory on the black market, and it's a serious matter, *compañero* Osorio, what d'you think; very serious, says I, and the worst of it is he's passed on the tip to the other *compañeros* and a lot of them want to sell their quotas, and we reckon it's not on, *compañero*, and I ask them, how'd this happen, I've always thought *compañero* Oliva was on the left, that he'd always been with us; and they say, that's right, but this is how things are now, and what do you reckon on it, *compañero* Osorio; what can I say, it's terrible; well, the leading *compañeros* here want to kick him out but we on the Committee don't have it in us to do that, and think that we can't go around kicking people out, much less anyone from our own class, see *compañero*, and if we tell the official in charge they'll have him out before his feet can touch the ground, and it was only a month ago his wife had their first kid, and how's it seem to you, *compañero* Osorio;

what d'you want me to say, says I; tell us, please, 'cos El Negro doesn't want anything to do with it, 'cos he says that if they pick on Oliva everyone'll be saying it's his fault, Secretary Negro's fault; shit, some fine mess you're dumping on me, *compadres*, what am I supposed to do?; well, talk to the *compañero*, and decide; but, *compañeros*, I say; tell Oliva to come in, he's waiting outside; what, he's outside the door! says I, shivering, Marita, with a bigger shiver than your Fats himself, a shiver too big for me to take, Marita; and so, come in, *compañero* Oliva, they say, and leave, closing the door behind them, and Oliva's left there in front of me with the little hair he's got all messed up, his tools hanging from his belt, his thin moustache wet with frost, and blowing on his hands as if pretending to be a steam engine, and me there in front, totally and utterly in front of the *compañero*; and I'll tell you something, when I saw the bloke there in front of me, freezing, a bit hunchbacked, and smiling like the man-of-the-match, I didn't feel sorry for El Negro, nor for the President, nor even for this bugger himself, Mari, I felt sorry for myself, for Chrissake, felt sorry for myself because I was absolutely nobody, I didn't have any hard feelings towards Oliva, I wasn't in any party, I hadn't read a quarter of the stupendously proletarian books El Negro's read, and I felt sorry for myself because of all the *compañeros*, I, who wasn't anybody, I, for fuck's sake, Negro, I have to decide what was to be done about him, so let's see, *compañero*, I said, d'you know why they brought you here? sure, Osorio, I know, excuse me, Oliva, if I tell you what the *compañeros* are saying, because I don't want to offend, that's okay, *compañero* Osorio, that's why we're class comrades and proletarians, after all, exactly Oliva, what you've been doing goes against the class and against the proletariat, which is to say against the proletarian class; just a sec, *compadre* Osorio, what's this, are you calling me a class traitor (imagine the tremendous start I'd made, Mari, as soon as I opened my mouth I was in it up to my neck); not exactly, *compañero* Oliva, but without wanting to cause offence, can you explain to me yourself whether it's true that you've been selling your cloth quota on the black market; and *compañero* Oliva stands there looking as if someone had stuffed ice up his arse, staring at me as if to say, is *that* why they brought me here, for *that*, which is exactly what he says in the end, grinning from ear to ear: that's what the *compañeros* brought me here for? and then, while Oliva cools off, I'm warming up; that's right, *compañero*, don't you reckon there's anything wrong with that? and Oliva says no, Osorio, I don't, because if I hadn't heard, if I wanted to know, the factory is ours now, belongs to its workers, isn't that right? so if each *compañero* has a quota of cloth it's up to him if he wants to leave it at home or sell it wherever he wants, that's why the factory is ours, and if you want to know something else, *compañero* Osorio, I reckon that the way things are going in this process we're all going to end up in the shit; and suddenly I feel as though a motor has started up inside me which is sorting everything out, I felt like I was a fat guy who could work fine when my engine's warmed up, like an old jalopy, so I said, just a sec, *compañero* Oliva, and now I was saying *compañero* Oliva sort of half suspicious-like, just a sec *compañero* Oliva, would you like to explain that again; it's dead simple, *compañero* Osorio, the factories are handed over to the workers, and sure, I say, agreed, and what else, *compañero*, so this factory here should be ours, if we own the machinery; and me mute so far, sure, completely agreed, what do you want me to say, Negro; so, fine, I say, is it ours or isn't it? do the ninety one nationalised factories belong to the people, or not? and Oliva says, no, sir! the people's they are not, 'cos he's from the people and he's not getting any of the factory's money; and that was when I really saw the bloke, saw him as if I had him in that ray machine at the doctor's, without a stitch on him, had him figured right down to the last toenail; so I sat on the desk, with my eyes fixed on him and not shifting them from him again, and with all my fears about the thing gone, and finished with the niceties, as they say, and said to him: know what, Oliva? you're no traitor, you're no deserter from the cause of the proletariat; do you know what you are? you're a poor bastard! what did you say, *compañero*? what I said, mate, is that you are a poor bastard; hold on there, *compañero*, respect is respect; now don't get me wrong, Oliva, what I said I said, and I meant it, but what you want, man, is that all the workers become capitalists, man, you, the owner of this, want to compete with the other capitalist who owns that, and if possible you'd like to have workers to work for you when you get rich, isn't that right, man, because if we carried on like that the copper miners, the copper miners, man, would have to be the owners of the mines, and be paid in dollars, and drive around in Cadillacs and have apartments in Miami, and their kids would go to school in London, and they'd even have their own private army; and d'you know what, Oliva? you carry on like this because you're ignorant, because you don't understand what the struggle of the people is all about, because you don't understand that you yourself are a poor bastard, because when you sell your bit of cloth on the black market, you're selling your kid, man, because you're pushing everything backwards, and you're carrying on worse than the reactionaries, worse than the *milicos* when they raid us, worse than the fascists when they shoot us up, because you're breaking up the only weapon we

have, man, our class morality, our class consciousness, gettit, mate? and Oliva stares at his boots and
doesn't even raise his eyes when he says, but don't
get so worked up, *compañero*; and I say, really worked
up I'm not, but I want to know if you understand;
and Oliva wipes his hand down his face and I can see
that what he wants to do is hide his eyes but instead
of that, as he sees I'm still looking at him, he goes
over to the window and pretends to be looking outside, but what can he look at outside when the shut-
ters have been closed since the night before because
the fascists go about spraying off machine gun bursts
at anyone who takes a breath of air, and I guess that
Oliva is like that because Oliva is a good guy really
with his heart in the right place, and I know what he
must have just above his boney cheeks at that
moment, and because I know that you don't watch a
man while he's shitting, I sit down to read the paper,
the red one which tells things like they are, until *compañero* Oliva turns round and says to me: anything
else, *compañero*? and I don't say anything, so, right,
then, I'll be going, and I say, sure, and as soon as he
leaves in come El Negro and the boys from the Committee with their faces like the biggest question mark
you ever saw, so I say sit down, and explain things to
them blow by blow and act everything out, everything he did and everything I did, and the *compañero*
militants sat there, their gobs open like ventilators
and their faces neither one thing nor another, as if the
three of them were in a colour photo the whole while,
and at least they blinked or I might have thought the
*momios* had got them with a freezing ray, until by the
end the one who had the face like a question mark
must have been me, and more than a minute went by
like that and all I did was to light up a cig, and then in
the end El Negro got up with a grin like I'd never
seen, a smile which showed off his whole set of white

teeth like a horse's, and he came over and said: fucking brilliant, Fats, and the other *compañeros* got up and shook my hand as if I was at death's door, and me, Marita, 'cos I'm the kind of geezer who always comes out with the sob-words, the only thing it occurs to me to say is: *venceremos*!

As he crossed the living-room, he saw standing in front of the piano, as if before a stormy ocean, Corporal Sepulveda, in uniform, complete with revolver and service boots. He had his hat on as well, and from behind seemed to be listening to some message whispered to him by the piano. Don Manuel found something expectant in his attitude, and crossed to the stairs on tiptoe so as not to involve him in a conversation in which he would feel obliged to cheer him up and make him venture confidences which would later make him blush and after which perhaps the Corporal would not come down to eat for a week.

He sat down on the inside edge of the bed and from there pressed the lamp switch. The light spread together with the youth's ample yawn.

"How goes it, Arturito? How's it coming along?"

"How d'you do, Don Manuel."

"Well, thanks. How's the football going, boy?"

"Fine, I guess. One trainer's talking about the States. There's a college there which wants to form a major team, and they want Latin Americans for it. They pay in dollars, see." He yawned again, and rubbed his eyes. "After the rent, are you?"

"No, son. I'm not here for that. Come here."

"What's up?"

"I've something to show you. Something I've brought with me."

The youth sat up, putting his bare feet on the floor, and Don Manuel extracted a red leather-bound book from under his arm.

"That's what you brought?"

"Here, Arturito, are very pretty things to say to the ladies."

The young man scratched his head as if shaking off his sleep, and rubbed his thighs, glimpsing in the mirror the little smile that appeared on his lips.

"To a lady," he repeated. "Don't think that'll be of much interest to me, Don Manual. I don't want to talk to them. You know what it is I want."

"That's just the problem, boy. You're too forward. D'you know the author?"

"Neruda." He looked up from the book to its owner's face. "Pablo Neruda? The poet?"

"I want you to listen to something. Then you'll see the pretty things there are here to say to the ladies!"

"Has good chicks, does he, this poet?"

With a meaningful glance, Don Manuel indicated the size of the book.

"Any number," he said, opening at the page where the ribbon cut between the Bible-thin paper of the complete works.

"He's very important, Pablo Neruda," said Arturo. "Won the Nobel Prize."

"Right. Now, listen to this, boy—"

> For my heart your breast is all,
> for your freedom my wings are all.
> From my mouth will reach the sky
> all that slept upon your soul.
>
> In you is the day's first hope.
> You come like dew to the corollas.
> You subvert the horizon with your going.
> Ever in flight like the wave.
>
> I have said that you sang in the wind
> like the pines or like the masts.
> Like them you are tall and taciturn.
> And suddenly sad, journey-like.

*Welcoming as an ancient road,*
*you are peopled by echoes and familiar voices.*
*I awoke and sometimes they migrate and flee*
*the birds that were sleeping in your soul.*

Don Manuel finished reading, and smoothed the fine page with his palm. Without looking at Arturo, he let the silence deepen and deepen—that absence of words which is the triumph of the poet, uniting and remaining unspoken. He felt its presence in his very eyes, in the soft trembling which tingled in his blood. Then, looking up from the book, he saw that Arturo was absorbed in watching the ceiling, his head propped against the wall.

"Did you understand?" he said gently, as if his strong voice were wrapped in velvet. "That's how to speak to a young lady." Arturito continued staring at the roof, without even moving his eyelashes. "What d'you say, boy? What are you thinking?"

Arturo inhaled deeply, and said: "How much money is the Nobel Prize worth?"

The landlord leapt off the bed, slammed the book shut and within one second had the door open. From there he flung the book onto the bed.

"There's going to be a Grand Fiesta on Saturday, my boy. If you want to make a start some day, you'd better start reading books like that."

When Don Manuel had disappeared, Arturo gave vent to a wide yawn which sent him rolling from one side of the bed to the other. Under the lamp, he flicked through the pages of the book as if shuffling playing cards. Suddenly he stopped and began to read from a random page:

*Kiss me bite me burn me,*
*for I come to land*
*only by the shipwreck of my male gaze*
*in the boundless waters of your female eyes.*

He looked up and kept listening to the inner sound of the words.

"Bite me, burn me," he chewed intensely, putting all of his lips, all of his teeth, all of his tongue and all of his throat behind the words. He punched himself on the knee. "Bite me, burn me," he said in his natural voice. Then: "Now, *that's* a poem!"


When Don Manuel reached the bottom step, he saw the Corporal's silent back at the piano. This time he delivered a firm kick to the round table and shouted at Sepulveda:

"Come on, man, play that piano! Play it! What do you think you're doing?"

The Corporal spun round on his heels, remote from anything like a jump, almost treading air, almost as if he did not exist. His brown face, always so correctly shaven, displayed the shadow of a beard, and the neck of his uniform was open, exactly as in those films where the soldier is disgraced and there's a tremendous roll of music and the fellow lowers his head and his fiancée marries another. But there was no trace of the tears in Sepulveda's eyes, no desperation, and he was almost smiling, though a little sadly.

"We're confined to quarters, Don Manuel," he said. "Something's up."

The landlord approached the piano, inviting him with a gesture. "Come on, man. Play us something."

The Corporal dried his hands on the serge of his uniform and with grand panache played thirty perfect seconds of "For Elise", plunging his fingertips onto the keys in such a way that the vibrations of the strings rang ever louder around the entire boarding house. When he had finished, he placed his fingertips together as if praying. But that wasn't it.

"Is it the coup?" said Don Manuel, without looking at him.

"Looks like it."

"Tomorrow?"

"Maybe."

The Corporal stood up, looked sideways at the door, and led Don Manuel by the arm behind the piano. There he suddenly plunged his hand into his cartridge pouch and, asking Don Manuel to put out his hand, filled it with ammunition and closed it himself, enclosing the bullets.

"Just so you know, I'm only keeping this one," he said, loading his revolver. "And so you also know, it's for me, just in case."

He looked his host in the eye, and made a comic gesture with his eyebrow, like Cantinflas or someone.

"Just in case," he repeated.

Señor Lecaros: you look a swell, extremely slick, swanky, lofty and artistic, classy, dandy and brilliant, the suit courtesy of General Electric and the hair up there with Gardel, so smooth you could be a bullfighter or an admiral or the owner of a yacht, we're all overwhelmed by your show, if we'd known you were coming like this there'd have been no need to arrange an orchestra, you shine so loudly, so extravagant, so lavish, and those gold sequins swimming on your jacket almost blot out the collection of beauties here on the stage in their little white dresses and bunches of carnations, as if all princesses were brides, and all of us going crazy for their lips painted up with that moist rouge the little darlings use and who would say seeing them now, the little sweethearts floating in their proud percale, skirts gliding past us, that these were the same girls Thursday afternoon around five leaving the factory with their empty lunch boxes eyes already asleep skin smudged with that dust, that fluff which floats all day and all night on the shop floor like savage white beasts, who would believe it the proud, the lovely as princesses that they shine on the stage, their little breasts all arranged neat and tiaras of tiny silver beads sparkling on their foreheads, and the youngest of all with her black eyes fixed, her belt just above her shins and that's *compañera* Emilda Espinoza, 17 years old and already a leader in the Southern Region, as you'll find out, Señor Pequeño, smiling all to herself the little sweetheart, it's her who's signalling to us, and him at table 15 is Emilda's dad, miner until he was fifty-five, which is the same as saying crippled with silicosis, who said on the anniversary of the nationalisation of copper he'd buy a set of false teeth so we could appreciate his smile, look at him now, and he also said that he doesn't mind dying now because finally there's democracy in this country and the land is for those who work it and the nationalised factories will never be given up, Don Florencio Espinoza by name, 67 years old and 50 years a militant, and when Emilda was born he didn't want to baptize her Emilda, wanted to call her you'd never imagine what better not even to talk about it, and as far as I'm concerned she's going to be Queen 'cos the girl is like a daughter to the old 'uns and a sweetheart to the lads, she has everything, and three or four of them have wanted to marry her, but she says no way, why should she be stupid enough to have liberated herself with the process just to go and warm the sheets for some jerk who's all very fine in the shop with his "darlin'" here and "sweetheart" there, but afterwards at home with a bun in the oven they come on all tough and think of nothing but leaping into bed with a drink or two inside them and setting to making little *compañeros*, see?

What an unforgettable day, Señor Lecaros: you were impeccable, and believe me I still haven't the least idea where you stuck the egg, or how you lit up the cigarette on your bum, that was brilliant, Señor Lecaros, killing, and you always so serious over things, so professional in front of the people in your golden jacket and that's leaving aside Angel, which would be another story, wouldn't it, all dressed in white, the great fink, lovely, like he was the gallant of all the princesses, hair as slick as can be, and far be it from me to pry into professional secrets, but how much does a jacket like that set you back, ball-park figure like, considering the lace shirt with the frills, and those cuffs hanging down like a first communion jacket, and the velvet bowtie, more-or-less, *grosso modo*, Señor Lecaros, how much did you fork out, begging your pardon for the impertinence, knowing you never smile ever, which Angel says is a question of your style, and that you have a heart of gold and that your face just doesn't fit it, you're just naturally severe of feature, he says.

Señor Lecaros: fortunate are the eyes which behold and which beheld you in that gold jacket you're enough to make the mouth water, just imagine the teeth I could put in these gums with no more than the sleeve, today you're deluxe, a feast for the senses, ample, complete, magnetic and above all just perfect, perfect and thrice perfect, and I hope you'll excuse me but my son and daughter-in-law and, well, begging your pardon.

Señor Lecaros: I'm seeing you, but I can't believe it, let me put on my dark glasses to appreciate the details, these buttons like emeralds, and all the rest, I just look at you and come over all giddy, you truly bring on the dizzies, isn't that so? genuinely magnificent, Cecil B. de Mille, Elizabeth Taylor in Cleopatra, what can I say, you bring style to the party, look at the kids with their go-go like a yankee musical, and it's all thanks to you, Señor Lecaros, that, how can I explain it, you gave the event pizzazz, made it special, see? very special, 'cos the other time a radio announcer came with no tie, see? a brown suit and no tie, if you get my meaning, very good, I'm sure, but depressing, right? The problem with the artists' union, you see, is they always send us proletarian blokes who dress like us, and that's no good at all, 'cos as you see we like the world of illusion, of fantasy, with a neon moon and birds all dressed up, lots of style, Don Lecaros, 'cos for realistic art we have the union, right? so all that's left for me is to congratulate you and wish you all the best and it looks like you're on.

And in the show too, Señor Lecaros, you walked as tall as your performance, not just your own height. When you went back to the stage one or two of them wisecracked, if you were a banana? or, from which tinware shop you had been bought, Don Mabrino they called you, but generally speaking, Don Lecaros, that ovation was unprecedented, and you got up there and took hold of the microphone, so serene, so professional, poker-faced, as perfect as that, and the lads from the unions gathered round and the dancing stopped and the drums rolled, beaten by the announcing Angel himself, until the cymbals and trumpet tremble in sympathy, and you lower your arm like an axe made of light, as if spilling honey from your fingers, and the combo "Satan" goes quiet and you at the microphone (which is where the men arrive and go over to Arturo at the bar while he's persuading them to put ice cream in his champagne and talking when he can to Susana and they ask him if that's Señor Lecaros and Arturo says yes and is it the same Señor Lecaros they call Señor Pequeño and Arturo grins at them not seeing anything strange about them and says yes, that's him, alias Señor Pequeño) with your cultured voice, like one of those grandees who's all pipe and cufflinks, taking our immaculate bride and saying *like a star, like a flower, Lucia Alba, from our neighbourhood*, and they applaud Lucia Alba who at six every morning except Mondays weighs out bread rolls by the kilo in the scales, the old women with their ration cards in hand pinching the ends to see they're nice and warm, the same Lucia Alba one and only much-loved entrant from the Bakers' Union, and they all applaud her, but the bakers most of all of course, and you applaud too with your magician's hands, Señor Lecaros, and as you do so your jacket lights up and contracts like an accordion of gold and wind, prettier than a poem, sir, and now you've quietened them down with a circle of two fingers which you bring down from your forehead to your chest while you sssshhhh with perfect clarity into the microphone, and the next presents herself with her glorious bust representing the textile workers and smiling the cheeky smile of a lass who's game and blushing as usual because she knows all the *compañeros* value her for her contribution to the union but that now they're having a party they're not going to miss the single and sublime opportunity of gazing at those tits which, while we're on the subject, it must be said we haven't seen the like of in the neighbourhood for quite some time, round as dutch cheeses, and you, Señor Lecaros, with your instinct for the grand gesture, for hitting the mark with the right grand words, say with such aptness, such charm, such transparency and such unforgettableness: *From the depths of the sea, this star appeared, her eyes shining black as can be, cut from the rocks below. Her soul is a siren's, with lovely form adorned, her beauteous eyes are two, and other pretty things also are two*, and the star blushes a little more, but more than getting angry she's enjoying it all because no one had ever said such pretty things about her endowments, and the boys from the factory couldn't have said it better themselves, we couldn't have said it better ourselves, Señor Lecaros (and meanwhile you didn't know that the men bought a drink for the footballer, chatted with him about this and that, saying he's not bad, is he, that presenter, not half bad, right, and one redhead, very George Raft, says to the other, reminds you of a friend of ours, a mate of ours, don't he, sucking his *cuba libre* through his teeth, the ice dancing against his tongue, and the footballer not giving a damn, not interested in the life of the dwarf or his Frankenstein, hanging around all day long with his chicken and they even say he gets up to all kinds of filth with the bird, and the redhead says what's all that about a chicken, and Arturo cheers, down the hatch, that chicken who's always pissed and gobbling corn and massacring worms in the backyard, and the men now watch Señor Pequeño's act intently, thumbs behind their lapels, very Humphrey Bogart the both of them, very interesting, don't you think, oh very) and you, Señor Lecaros, untiring on the stage and the workers clapping and you, always high art but now flying higher, bringing over the beauty with the belt and, purring into the microphone like a pampered cat, your cultured voice carressing the *s*'s, the *d*'s powerful like explosions, and the *t*'s like small daggers, flatter and coo over Flor Maria Fernandez, reciting with every particle of your being *as there are subtle flowers, and there are others from the field, so there is one Flor Maria Fernandez, who adorns the union* and then the graceful sweep with which you lead her to the other side of the stage and the careful pause as you wait for the ovation to die down in its own time, and the whole act of presentation has its own rhythm, and its own charm, it's your gala night, Señor Pequeño, your golden moment in show business history, and there you go *teeth like pearls, lips of ruby, Teresa Lopez, from Carafi's Footwear*, and you, impeccable, stellar, sanctified and approved by all, admired and idolised, Señor Lecaros, with your sensitive and infinitely tiny finger on her waist as it's *the sun is the joy of the day and the moon the sun in the night, and Blanca Ximena Perez illuminates the workers at Rocher* (and you didn't know that the Beast was glowing in the garden made frost in his albion suit and in the heart of this white night the cock was warming his chest like sparks, and the Beast peeped at it, a dream-figure like a meteorite, a slow and bulky comet, and Juana Gomez wound her thirty-five years up in her braids and remembered another night in the Caupolican, before she embarked upon her career as a domestic maid, when there was a certain other man in a white suit like this, a man who was called Perez Prado whose jacket was too big for him like a priest's vestments down to his knees from which emerged legs of butter gliding mambo-mambo-mambo and holding her hand in the gallery of the Caupo not her first boyfriend, but the third, but the first who'd done it with her, maybe the one she'd liked least, but there you are ... and she also watched the cock on the Beast's breast and she felt something both passing and permanent, and Juana Gomez felt that there in the backyard there were no more glasses to wash, that the broom had turned to dust, that the clots of garbage melted away like jelly in the warmth of the night, that tonight all the photos on the posters from *Wave* magazine were coming alive and nestling by her ear whispered to her *Juanita, you're eternal*, and then words came from her mouth, words that said: when I was little I had a cavy, a little cavy no bigger than a mouse, and spent all day long with him, I was going to school so I took him with me, in his shoebox, and he was as white as can be, so white that I had nightmares that I'd lose him in the *cordillera* and never find him again, and I loved the poor little thing so much; and the Beast raises himself a little in the night like a ghost and can hardly see the pupils in Juana's dark eyes and says I guess he's dead by now, and Juana says that's right, they killed the poor little fellow, and the Beast comes closer and takes her hand like that of an actress in the films and now yes he can see her eyes a little better because she turns her head and the moon catches her face, and the Beast says don't be sad because maybe the cavy will revive, and she squeezes his hand and behind her there is like a bodyguard of stars who make the scene live for ever, there they all are Ginette Acevedo, Palmenia Pizarro, Ramon Aguilera, Sandro, Yaco Monti, Leonardo Favio, Javier Solis, Lucho Gatica, Enrique Guzman, Ernesto Gil Olivera with his Talking Organ, and Juana Gomez, the eleven immortals suspended in the breeze like a calendar where there are only holidays and nobody ever tears off the days, always shining, because the wind is warm and is always sweeping and sweeping, but without a broom, shining and shining, but without wax, washing and washing, and without water, and there's only one who's there but isn't in the photo of the eleven immortals, who's out of it, but at the same time is sort of in it because all he does in space is gaze at the eleven and among them more than any at Juana Gomez, and this man for Juana Gomez is a knight with the body of a god and the face of Miguel Romero Ortiz, currently graphical worker and father of two children who go to university, husband of a woman who isn't her, Juana Gomez, but is rather Angelica Estevez, the grocer's niece, the same Miguel Romero Ortiz who gave her her first romantic kiss, her first kiss with the tongue, but who respected her and never made her his because he was always a gentleman and only the things of life came between them, maybe love as fragile as crystal, fate which is cruel with those in love, or simply the layer of time which with its icy hands freezes passion, I don't know which or maybe all of them thought Juana Gomez in a second which was also eternal as she answered the Beast, and what a shame that although he held her hand the Beast wasn't in the photo of the eleven immortals all smiles and arranged like a football team, and she replied to the Beast: God willing my little pet will revive because I love him terribly, and at the same time tried to put a bit of grass in the cock's beak, eat up, little fellow, and the Beast felt her hand as soft as

a warm bird between his fingers and he asks her when
did it happen, when did you lose your dear little cavy,
and she says when I was little, and he looks at his
chicken as if he were reading the idea there and says
don't worry because things which happened a long
time ago go on existing, because existence is divided
into the visible and the invisible, and things go from
one side to the other, and that's all there is to it, and
that explains to you Juanita the mystery of life and
death, and Juana says: lovely, Angel, it's very beautiful what you say and asks if he knows what he's just
told her if he knows also whether what you think and
imagine also exists over there, and suddenly will be
real and not just pure thought, and the Beast says:
no, Juanita, I can't say that because I don't know,
but do you know what, I'm ashamed that I've got
this chicken and you've lost your cavy, and she says:
no, Angel, don't be silly, it was a long time ago, it'd be
the same as crying over Don Pedro Aguirre Cerda
dying, see, Angel, I swear it doesn't matter at all that
they killed the cavy, and says Angel: promise? and
Juana Gomez, more and more moon on her eyelids,
promise!) and you still don't know, because Juana
Gomez hasn't yet come in with her hands to her temples screaming, because everyone's waiting for you
to receive the envelope with the jury's verdict, and
the envelope passes from hand to hand and you blink,
Señor Lecaros, as the little object flutters before your
eyes, lending colour and sublimity to the moment,
and you put out your arm and now any moment we'll
know who is Queen, and despite it all you don't
change, you don't waggle your buttocks like that Don
Francisco on the telly every time he presents anything
to anyone, you are just *there*, Señor Pequeño! with
your ineffable technique, perfect, just right, sharp as
ninepence, waiting for the envelope to reach you, and
only one thing do you allow yourself, something which

makes the spectators piss themselves laughing and the bosoms of the contestants quiver with nerves, and this that you do, Señor Lecaros, is to look at the girls with your eyebrows raised while you adjust your bowtie and then fix the workers from all the unions with the same look as if you were Robert Mitchum receiving a poisoned letter from the cable that hangs from the heavens, you're completely absorbed in this, Señor Lecaros, and only knew afterwards when Emilda Espinoza was already Queen and the *compañero* Under-Secretary of Labour who has come to honour us with his presence has taken her to dance on the waves, and Juana Gomez comes in with her hands to her temples, and Don Manuel pushes his way through to the garden scattering the dancers to all sides, with El Negro running behind him, and you feel that your apotheosis and your damnation have happened both on the same night (how were you to know, Señor Lecaros, that the redheads had fallen on the garden like a cartload of carrots, the moon glinting off their knives, how were you to know if at that very moment Emilda Espinoza raised her arm, not like a queen, but with her fist high like a socialist and her smile like everybody's sweetheart, like a queen who was queen but more than a queen the *compañera* of the anniversary, and the drums and guitars struck up the march and everybody was singing *Venceremos*! the bakers singing, and Calafi's Footwear singing, and the textile workers singing, until the Under-Secretary floating on the waves with *Queen Emilda Primera*, which were the last words he spoke into the microphone because Juana Gomez was clinging to his trousers, they're going to murder Angelito, help him, and the redheads crouching in the garden with their knives out straight and Angel, turned into a snowman in the middle of the night, pressing the chicken to his heart and the small redhead saying softly give

131

it here, and the big redhead, come on, my lad, it's ours, and the cock sparking away like a firework, and the back of Angel's left hand dripping a trickle of blood, and give it here, I'm telling you, give it to me, you shit, give it over if you don't want a red sash on that real slick suit, big fella, and Angel panting, dizzy in a circle of knives, helpless without his hands, and here comes Don Manuel onto the patio, and Fats and El Negro as well, with Arturo and Susana peeping out and the redheads spin the knives round towards them and stay there as alert as athletes, and it's Don Manuel who steps forward and it's he who speaks, saying do you have a problem, gents, something not to your liking, some uncivil look, some naughty word, the redheads nothing like that, mister, we've just come for what's ours, what the big fella has cuddled in his chest is our cock, and our best cock at that, and Don Manuel says now just a minute, let's take this step by step, were you gentlemen invited to the party, no, mister, and Don Manuel, then do you gentlemen belong to any union, do you have any union card, or some credential you can show us, polite, Don Manuel, like a bank manager, and the redheads no, but... and Don Manuel looks round at everyone, at Fats and Arturo and El Negro and the baker-princess and the boys who by now are hanging on the door and elbowing each other as they peer out into the garden, would any of you know these gentlemen, by sight or by reference, and seeing as nobody says anything but just move their heads from left to right, Don Manuel walks over to the redheads, shakes their wrists and the knives are on the ground, and with all due respect, gentlemen, and no offense, gentlemen, this is a respectable dance and we'll show you the way out, this way, gentlemen, and the crowd divides, and from the doorway the small redhead says, tell the dwarf and the big fella that the next time it'll be guns, no more knives, got it? Tell the big one not to forget it, and Don Manuel gives them an amiable push then closes the door and through the little hole which is left half-open, I'll pass on the message with pleasure and good night, and by the time he returned to the patio some-one had already said *nothing happened here, okay*, so Don Manuel said it in vain because everyone was back on the dancefloor, everyone that is but for a small gentleman in a gold jacket, hair-raisingly lavish for the neighbourhood, faithful replica of the stars cir-cling in space, erect in his knife-edge creased trousers, that's to say that professional gent of the first rank who that night had achieved the pinnacle of popular-ity, the benediction and praise of hundreds upon hun-dreds, and who now accompanied by his immaculately besuited partner crept along the outside wall of the hall to lose themselves in the ignominy of the night.

She decided to let her eyes go dreamy, saying to her-self with a smile that to be realistic about it, every time that happened she started thinking of people as better than they really were. What's more, the kids were playing Lucho Zapata and the Machine's ver-sion of Jaime Atria's "I've a heart that would die for you", which had become her favourite *bolero* after she'd heard it at the fiesta in November 1970 around the fountain outside the President's palace, when the girls could no longer resist the love in the air and had danced *boleros* buried in the *compañeros'* arms, and she had danced with the writer *compañero* who'd been on the jury at the Casa de las Americas and already that night they'd talked about the need to set up creative workshops in the shantytowns, and about everything that was happening having to hap-pen again, recreated and reinvented a thousand times over in literature, cinema, songs, murals, book

**133**

clubs, fashion and even, he'd said, in the way we *compañeritos* are growing these succulent moustaches, isn't that right, Susana? and right there he'd written her a poem on a paper napkin from the Indianapolis Bar and the poem had been called UPOEM and all it did was describe the girl's teeth as they danced to "I've a heart that would die for you" and then copied out word for word the lyrics, "I've a heart that would die for you, if only you would give it love", and at the end he'd written his name, which was Antonio, and there it was, one poem, signed and sealed he'd said, d'you like it, or not? And, well, she Susana had always thought it would be great to appear in a poem, but not stuck in amongst the lyrics of a *bolero*, because although she liked *boleros* as *boleros*, and poetry as poetry, she didn't much like the two things being mixed up, 'cos it was like mixing wine and milk, though in fact that *specific poem, that* one in particular, she liked though she'd have liked the poet to say it really *was* a poem, I mean one that could be published an' all that, and the writer said sure, why not, and that himself he liked it just as it was because like that it was a political poem because at the beginning the date was clearly noted, and she hadn't noticed that, had she? and it tells what the people like you and I are feeling, get it, Susana? the little thing going on here is also liberation, look in the people's eyes, don't they all seem to you to be looking at each other like lovers? well, that's liberation too, and afterwards she would remember that she'd told him that if that were modern poetry then writing poems was a doddle, and anyone in the neighbourhood or the factory could write poems like that 'cos the people there have very good hearts and good feelings and that even she herself could write a poem like that, and right there in the Indianapolis, drinking pilsener (well, in fact, as well as the writer there were some *compañeros* from the Pedagogico, but as she'd been talking to the writer, tough luck that's all, she could only remember him), the writer said that's right, *compañera*, that's exactly the point, now the writers are all going to go everywhere so no word stays unwritten, but she shouldn't imagine that it was as simple as all that, that writing a poem was just a matter of keeping your pencil sharp and that's that, *il cuore va bene* and a spot of the romantics and bob's your uncle, but we must liberate expression, which is a kind of piquancy, Susana, which sometimes comes over us writers and we have a duty to teach it and stimulate everyone so everyone can write, and Susana remembered that Antonio was right because lots of times she'd wanted to write poetry, most of all when the truckers' strike had everyone fed up to here and she'd tried to write one about voluntary work, but it had come out all slushy and although the kids all said it was beautiful the fact is that it wasn't anything like that simple and amazing poem which the *compañero* writer Antonio had written in the Alameda and which later on was published in the cultural magazine *Fifth Foot*, and from then on every time she made her eyes go dreamy, Susana thought about the woman in the poem being her in person and nobody in the world knowing, and although it was a soppy thought she liked it to come to her and remind her at moments like this when the band played the same tune, and what's more it was the anniversary of the nationalisation of copper, and her *cuba libre* was slipping deliciously through her veins. And so she smiled. Smiled half over the writer who had written the poem and half again over Lucho Zapata and the Machine, and then she lowered her head with a little laugh, because that had also been the glorious day when Luisin Landaez had missed a step during his *cumbia* and as he'd come to earth the stage had given way, and the black guy had fallen straight through, but with that delicious Colombian cool carried on singing with nothing but his head poking up from the stage and everybody in tears with laughter and afterwards Landaez, who's no fool when it comes to business, composed the *cumbia* "The Big Crash" which got higher up the hit parade even than "Macondo".

When the *compañero* came by with the tray, they chose *cuba libres*, but now the band was playing a different tune, and the silence now was different too and Arturo seemed far away. Susana smiled at him and he pressed her hand, very gently, perfectly tolerably, and said, "I love you". She stood up, somewhat amused, with a trembling in her neck and a sweet sensation in her knees and the warm scent of the night making her want to caress her own breasts, or love someone who would caress them for her. It amused her that Arturo should have said, "I love you", when everybody on a date said "I fancy you", and "I love you" was like something off the telly. When she stood up, she'd ended up leaning against a tree, her belly curved slightly outwards, and this was the zone Arturo's hands slipped over on their way to take hold of her hard buttocks.

"I love you," he repeated, his hot breath approaching her ear.

The girl pushed away his face and hands without meeting resistance. She looked at him bemused, her eyes intense, and a little drunk as if trying to make out who this man was who kept falling all over her like a juke box needle on the current hit disc.

"So you fancy me, do you? Why, how, where, since when?"

"I like the way you are. You're different."

"What d'you mean, different? What does that mean?"

"Different! Not like the rest!" he said, pointing

towards the dance hall and bringing his face closer once again.

"Why do you call me that? I want to be like all the others! D'you think I like it when you say that?"

"Don't get riled. I thought...."

"Oh, really? Where did you get that from, what you said?" The youth arranged the hair on his forehead and said nothing, but kept looking at her, with something near to a pout on his lips. Susana crossed her arms on her breasts, understanding clearly that to say what you are thinking is also a way of staring at someone. "Anyway, you don't know what love is!"

The youth's hand went to the knot of his tie.

"What are you trying to insinuate? That I'm a virgin?"

Susana sank back into the tree trunk, and tossed back her drink, as if there were no words or gestures left. She said:

"That's got nothing to do with it. You're an animal! Let's get back to the dancing, if you don't mind."

Arturo pressed against her with the whole of his body, flattening her, though he left his arm hanging free, as a sign of respect.

"Don't go!" he implored. Susana saw his lips only millimetres from hers and, anticipating the kiss, moved her head slightly. Arturo didn't kiss her. For a minute his breath played over her, but all he did was to cross his arms above her hair, and stay in that position, half crushing her and half propping up the tree. "D'you like poetry?"

"Sure."

"Patriotic or romantic?"

Without seeking out her eyes, more concerned with his memory than her lips, Arturo moistened his dry mouth with each of the verses:

*Welcoming as an ancient road,*
*you are peopled by echoes and familiar voices.*
*I awoke and sometimes they migrate and flee*
*the birds that were sleeping in your soul.*

He swallowed, and like a supple branch of the tree itself wound his hand behind her neckline until for the first time he touched the elastic and formidable skin of the girl's breast.

"Leave me alone!" she said.

But Arturo was held magnetically to that soft swelling, and first placed his lips on hers, then pressed his sex against her waist, rubbing up against her body like a wounded insect in the mud.

"Don't go, don't go," he panted, "please don't go."

And now his forehead bumped once and again against hers as if he intended forcing his head into hers, filling her brain physically with his image, and perhaps it was to achieve this that he said, "I want you to love me, I want you to love me," so fiercely, with such violence that Susana felt her body no longer able to take in air, and under her hair the bark of the tree scratching the skin until it bled.

"Please," was the last Arturo said before, at the point of suffocation, she found his balls with her knee and doubled him up. His hands covered his groin, which filled with all, almost every last drop, of the matter of his dreams, the packed hold of a ship without a port, its coralline and explosion, its pigeons and rats, as if an uncontrollable surge, ebb and flow together, had fused into a single wave of pleasure and pain, and the cry which mounted his spine never left his mouth, and his unconscious hands were no more than a warmish, whitish vessel, no more than that—this was what went though his mind—once again, no more than that, and now it took no effort to let himself fall, and he landed face down on the earth pressing against the dry grass upon which fell a star-filled night, annointing it like a final breast, a condemned prisoner's pillow, and so he let everything that was left in him flow into his trousers, and the warm earth was cooler than his face and against it his forehead calmed again, and Susana had crouched against the tree, stroking her knee, submerged in her own outrage, gulping down the air in the patio and gingerly feeling at the damp cut which had split her hair, mixing her fingers in the blood on her scalp. Like a groggy boxer, she detached herself from the tree and stepped over him as if over a torn letter from an old love, which holds neither meaning nor nostalgia. Arturo felt her steps towards the dance hall but had no wish to raise his head. He wanted to see neither the soft texture of the sky, nor the leafy profiles of the shrubs, nor the symmetrical perfection of the moon. Even less did he want to see them now that his volcano was all lava, and his lava clotted and fused with the earth, from which earth, and from which night, nothing would ever come, and although the youth felt a new burst more liquid than the last coming over him, as if his whole body was a laboratory for witchcraft and terrors, he decided to seal every pore, melt into whatever was left inside him, poison himself within it, whatever it was, and there on the ground, nose in the grass, he encouraged himself with a smile and said to the soft night and the indifferent stars and the busy insects and the moon and the plants and the murmuring foliage of the tree: this is how I am, motherfuckers, and if you don't like it, you can go suck!

The gents' room emptied hurriedly as the lads rushed back to the hall. The romantic turn was next, with songs from the San Remo Festival, and none of them wanted to find their dates smooching with some other *compadre*, however decent he might be. Only Fats was left behind, taking off his jacket and letting his sweat flow as if he himself were a shower or a spring. Then he came across Arturo, langorously combing his hair in front of the mirror in the corner.

"How's things, Arturito?"

"So-so."

"Such is life," said Fats, removing his tie and turning the water on full. He studied the tantalizing jet, then bent down to offer it his head.

"Some life in this neighbourhood, in these unions," said Arturo, drying his comb on his lapel. "Stale cakes, pâté rolls, warm *cuba libres*." But Fats couldn't hear him, as his neck was receiving the benediction of the water and the sound sprayed round the room. As he tried to dry himself, Arturo stood beside him and watched him with concern in the mirror.

"The third anniversary march is coming up soon, Arturito. This time you have to come along, 'cos everyone has to be there. There has to be a lot of people to show the *milicos*, 'cos things are getting hot."

"Maybe." He scratched his cheek and offered Fats his comb the better to shape his forelock. "Hey, Fats, mind if I ask you something which has me wondering —no offense meant."

"Sure."

"No offense, really, Fats, but how did you hook that chick? I mean, talking straight, you're only so-so, aren't you? How can I put it—you cast a broad shadow, don't you? So, how'd you get a chick as tasty as that? If you follow my drift."

Fats took his time about extracting a mirror from his pocket. He breathed on it, rubbed it on the thigh of his trousers and put it in the footballer's hands, so he could comb himself with attention.

"Eh, Fats?"

"Speaking frankly, I reckin I 'catch the chicks' because I don't go around asking bloody silly questions like you, *compañero*."

Arturo blinked, and carefully followed the technique with which the fat guy set about fashioning his hair. Just like Elvis.

"What I'm on about, Fats, is just how you picked up *that* chick."

"Maria's her name, mate. Maria, not 'chick'."

"Maria, then."

"Because before her I had other girlfriends."

"Others?"

"Others, Arturito. Surprised?"

"But they must have been pretty niffy. Tubby like, that kind of thing."

"Let me show you some photos. Come into the light."

He took out his wallet, put the first photo into the palm of his hand, and placed it in front of the youth's nose.

"Who's that geezer?" he asked.

"My dad."

"He's as gross as you."

"*Was* as gross, mate. They killed him in November '62. Remember the massacre in the J M Caro shanty?"

"Can't say I do."

"Well, that's something else you need to get girlfriends: a decent memory." He passed over two photos of girls smiling for posterity. "Laurita Boisier— her parents were French. Ana Parra, folk singer." He put the third to his lips, and touched it with them. "Angelica de Osorio, my old lady."

"The three of them are really tasty! But it's Maria I'm on about Fats. How did you chat her up? How did you approach it? Waltzed up, opened your mouth and Jack's the lad? That's what I want to know!"

"Maria is the woman of my life, son. We met during the 1970 campaign. We had to go with the *cordillera* branch to spray wall slogans in the posh district, so we had to go out before dawn when it was so cold, man, that a *compañero* who took a slash froze his goolies. I'd danced with Maria once before at a party in the neighbourhood, but that time she'd been kind of dry and distant, snooty. But that night everything went as if we'd had it scripted. The wind whipped past us in the truck like in that kids' game—'here comes a chopper to chop off your head'—and we were like Spaniards shaking castanets, with the racket our teeth were making, and those who could were cuddling up together against the sideboards, and one of those who could was darlin' Maria, and when we came up against that wind that slaps against you in the Costanera she said to me, 'ooooh, it's cold', and while she said it she was already looking at me like she looks at me now, you've seen that look she gives me and nobody else, haven't you? well, it was like the tree bringing fruit to the table, mate, and so I put my arm round her shoulder, and that freezing wind blew straight up my armpit, but too bad, *compadre* 'cos side-on to the wind like that it hurts your eyes and there was no chance of closing them 'cos we had to watch out for walls decent enough to paint, or for cops, or whether the *momios* were coming, clubs 'n all, and suchlike, and at the same time as all that I was holding her tight from behind—tight, tight—hugging her warmly, lovingly, and 'okay?' I said, with the voice all husky, see, so she could hear it came from deep down. 'Fine', she said, and nuzzled up against my shoulder with her face and hair, total ecstasy, man, and I could feel that if I stretched out my fingers a little more I could fit all her breast into my hand, and began to work my wrist round, eager as anything, the dirty lad, and it seemed as if I was

142

catching a bird 'cos of the way it was pulsing, and I had my hand right there like a dish, all ready to touch her and die right there, but I hardly moved forward at all, well brought up, gettit, repressive bourgeois morality, see? so there I was, neither one thing nor the other, shall I chance it or not, when she, in person, man, live and in the flesh, man, eased her breast into my hand and pushed herself forward. Did you ever hear the angels sing, mate? I did right there, boy, and afterwards she offered me her hair for me to kiss, and there I was nibbling it all, and then we rubbed noses and I swear I didn't even know her name, we all called each other *compañero*, and as I was about to ask her, the daft thing—and this is where I died, man—planted a kiss on me that you can never imagine, and at that time she was wearing her hair in a pony-tail, tied up with a ribbon, remember? and I buried my nose in that hair and said 'if we win in the election we could get married', and she took out a hand, right there in the North Pole, her little claw, and stroked my hand slowly and I realised she wanted to tell me I was okay, a fat boy who was fine with her and I plunged my nose into her hair again and she kissed me again, and the two of us with our teeth iced up with cold.... And that night, the lot, Arturito. We sprayed five walls, went a couple of rounds with the fascists, and at dawn I took her for a coffee to the bicycle repair shop. And that's how it all began."

From halfway through the story Arturo had buried himself more and more in himself. Staring fixedly at the wall, he felt as if Fats' tale were a film shown in the neighbourhood flea-pit where he himself was the triumphant star, with technicolour, violins courtesy of Mantovani, the works.

"That's how it all began", sighed Fats, floating on the same spell.

Arturo sighed deeply, turned on the tap, watched it

run for a second, and turned it off again. He smiled very sweetly, and when he spoke his voice sounded very like the way he'd heard himself use it a minute ago on the screen. In that voice, he said:

"Very pretty, Fats. You certainly know how to talk pretty. Me, on the other hand, I'm terrible at the lip."

Osorio put his hand on his heart.

"It's not a question of lip, friend. It's a question of having it here when you say it. Gettit?"

The other heard him, while trying to soak himself, but more through the gesture than the words. But at that moment El Negro came in for a leak. So Arturo slapped Fats on the shoulder, and with one eyebrow raised, and the righthand corner of his lip slightly higher than usual, said to him, in his normal voice:

"Yeah, I get it. You drugged her with pure blarney, Fat Man!"

With my own eyes, no, but my *compadre* told me.
And that's the same as if it was me, because the
things you go through together mean your lives get
mixed together and at times I remember things without knowing whether it was me or my *compadre* who
lived them and my *compadre* tells me the same happens to him. We split up for reasons of temperament,
because my physique's like you see and because I
prefer things quieter. On the other hand, my *compadre*'s tough and has a wilful, energetic streak; he
likes more action, and isn't even afraid of getting
shot at. That's how I ended up on traffic, and my
*compadre* Pedro joined the Palace Guard, six feet tall
and with that minister's bearing that demands respect, I'm telling you. We'd talked about what would
happen if one day what happened should happen and
my *compadre* had told me if it happened he'd do just
what he did do. My *compadre* told me the first thing
that came to his mind when he saw the tank crews
getting ready to blow holes in the Palace, in their
enormous helmets, wasn't what he would do when
the soldiers shouted "surrender, arsehole!" but was
what shitty luck it was that maybe he would have to
die on his Saint's Day, St Peter and St Paul's Day,
the great grief which would come over his wife when
he didn't come home, seeing as how she, his lady wife,
Paula Estevez, had invited me round for the traditional Saint's Day hotpot. My *compadre* says that he
said to himself: "We have to get out of this so as not
to let down my *compadre*." He's just like I'm telling

you, and if I didn't know him well, I wouldn't be telling you any of this.

And my *compadre* says that when things got to the stage of bullets flying in and out, they closed up the big door and put the bar across it and gathered together quickly, and the one who was captain said, "Right then, boys, you'll all have realised what's going on here; those outside want to overthrow the legal President, and the whole point of putting us here is in order to defend him, and as is my duty as captain here, my orders are that we get down to it, and how does that seem to you?" and everyone said orders is orders and we're here to obey them, and the captain said, "Very well, then, to battle stations and now we'll see if you remember what they taught you at police college!" And my *compadre* says that some colleagues weren't too keen on offering resistance, not because they weren't willing, but because they'd got wind that things were going to get hot and "We may wear uniforms but when it comes down to it we've all got wives and kids, and we always said if it's a choice between something happening and nothing happening then nothing's better". And the cannon fire was there to be heard right enough and that was enough to scare the pants off you, but what if the navy and the fliers turn up in the planes and the whole shebang turned a lot uglier, because if they didn't kill you here inside they'd shoot you outside. And the fact is the job's all very well when everything's peaceful and you pick up your wages in the middle of every month, but no amount of cash can compensate for what we, people of flesh and blood, suffer when the fat's really in the fire. Like my *compadre* says, in the service you think you're only visiting but really you're the prisoner.

And my *compadre* says after a while a bunch of lieutenants came over waving a white flag and shouting that they should hear them out before doing anything else because they had precise orders from their captain. And one of the lieutenants came in and asked who was in command, and that was the captain who had got down to it, not my *compadre* but the captain I told you about before, and he said "Here I am, that's me; what do you want, lieutenant?" "We're charged with informing you that the Palace Guard must surrender", and he goes on to say that his captain had ordered him to inform them that if the Guard left the building there'd be no more shooting and a truce would be declared, and our captain asked whose orders these were, in other words, where did these orders come from, and their lieutenant said they were orders from Captain So-and-So, and that his instructions were clear, and that in case they hadn't realised the tanks were outside and the army had risen and they were now in charge, and our captain says that may be so but their captain's orders are illegal and his lads are there to defend the legally constituted regime and he as a soldier should understand that duty is duty and if it falls to them to attack it falls to us to defend, and their lieutenant asks if that's all or if there is anything else, and my *compadre* says that our captain says no, that's not all, that there is something else, and that is that he can tell his precious captain that "The Guard never surrenders!" and according to my *compadre* their lieutenant left furious, and the tanks and soldiers began to fire and, sure, now everyone goes there to have a look and you can see the furrows they left, and all day long now people come out of curiosity and point out the holes with their fingers and seeing them now isn't anything, it's like when the storm's over and you can see the puddles in the street and you think, "Well, that wasn't so bad really", but my *compadre* says that when the captain said that it was as if the lads' spirits leapt and a glorious tingling came over them and all of them took up battle stations while the President spoke over the radio and said that the loyal troops were on their way and that the Guard was standing firm to defend itself.

And my *compadre* says that one of the Guard said there was something left to do, and everybody wanted to know what that something was, so there they were in the middle of the shooting asking him what was it that was left to do, and their colleague said that it wasn't much really, but that if the captain would permit he'd like to go up to the roof if it was possible to raise the flag because "if we're going to die it'll be defending our country and if my captain permits I propose raising the flag because that way it'll all be for ever, because while men may die history goes marching on, and what do you think, captain?" and our captain says very well, and that's fine, and he agrees, and is there a volunteer because as you can all see the bullets are flying, and the colleague says if it's a question of a volunteer then "here I am; I take responsibility for my own words", and the captain: "Then good luck". And my *compadre* says the colleague went crawling towards the roof, which in any case was dangerous enough as there were people shooting from the buildings, whether troops or God knows who, and that was how things were according to my *compadre*, and the sky was like one great cannon blast with the clouds all blotted out by smoke, and he thought "what will become of the boy if the Air Force suddenly attack?" while someone else said, "no, how can they attack a building right in the city centre?", that it was very dangerous, that they couldn't just turn up and start killing heedlessly, and my *compadre* says that when the fellow started to raise the flag there was a kind of flurry from man to man inside because they were all aiming at the soldiers and nobody could

**148**

look up at the roof but the word spread like wildfire, that the lad's up there, that the lad's unfolded it, that the lad's got it on the rope and now he's raising it, now it looks like he's been hit, no he seems okay, he seems to be dead, it seems all the fire is being concentrated on him and what if we loose off a broadside to cover him, and my *compadre* says he began to fire at whatever the machine gun was pointing at, which was just what had to be done in emergencies like this, and while the shots came at him the words went back and forth, how is he? he's done it—yes, it's all wrapped up, nobody had an eye to spare to look at the roof, nobody really knew, and in the end it was the fellow himself who brought the news, and I don't know his name nor would I want to mention it, who knows maybe some day they'll put it in the papers, or later, when things in the country are sorted out, they may put his name in the kids' books. My *compadre* says that if he didn't break down crying then it's only because he's never cried, and the soldier was there again and reporting to the captain that it's flying up above, captain, and the captain says very well, excellent, now let's see if we can get out of this alive. And in fact they did which is how my *compadre* could tell me all this.

But the most beautiful of all he told me, and I don't want to be political in what I tell you, Don Manuel, first because it's forbidden for professional reasons and second because you know I like to keep my nose clean, so what I'm telling you is no more nor less than what my *compadre* told me and my *compadre* said that in the evening all the people were in the square in front of the Palace all of them as pleased as kids because the loyal troops had won and the President, like Pedro, was home again and people were asking him to dish out some rough treatment right now to those who were to blame and many of the kids on the left were all ready to go and sort things out themselves but the President told them no, and that the strength of the people was in their prudence and reason, and when he talked about the people he said he wanted to mention one man so as not to mention hundreds and my *compadre* says he sent inside the Palace for the soldier who'd raised the flag to come out and greet the people and the lads said he should, and the man himself saying no, of course I can't, and the captain saying as well go on man, and my *compadre* says that the soldier said with your permission, then, captain, and only if you don't order me to stay put because this affects the whole Guard and not just me and shouldn't we just leave it as it is and why should we make a big thing of it, and the captain says look here, lad, it's the President himself asking, and the soldier says even so if it's all the same to you I prefer to stay here 'cos I'm just one of the Guard and if I did what I did well others did what they did too and that's my feeling about it, and the captain says very well if that's what you want we're not going to spend the whole night discussing it. And my *compadre* says the only thing he regrets is missing the party for St Peter and St Paul, because from then on they were confined to barracks, and when he told me all this he begged my pardon for the cock-up and wanted to know if the party had been a good one and how was his lady wife who I'd now got to know, and I said how do you think she is, nervous, and it was only at one in the morning that we drank a toast to you and it seems like you have Paula good and soft over you because she was as pale as a sheet the whole night long. And my *compadre* says it was the same for him because he spent the whole night thinking about Paula there in the dormitory in the Palace fed up at not being able to do what the President had said to the people from the balcony that they should do, that is go home and kiss their *compañeras*. And that was what my *compadre* told me.

Don Manuel refilled the glasses with Tarapaca ex-Zavala and waited in silence while Sepulveda drank it down and coughed to clear his throat. With a gentle movement he struck a match and lit a last cigarette. For a moment he watched the match hiss in the flame and only then took a sip from his glass. He attracted the Corporal's attention with a slight cough.

"And you, Sepulveda, how did you feel?"

The corporal rubbed his temples slowly and just remembered in time that he always had to count to three before answering such questions. Even more so now that his lips, his tongue, his eyes, his temples, his breath and a long and dewy story were all conspiring to form in his mouth the word: proud. So, he sighed and said:

"Well, Don Manuel, you know I'm not political."

Behind the heaps of garbage and skinny dogs, funereal pigeons and rusty cans, stretched a railway line. There they dropped, at their last gasp, and lay panting, faces to the sun, unable to control the palpitations of their hearts. Señor Pequeño lowered his eyelids and the first images of a dream began to take shape from out of a milky background. He had to sit up to avoid taking flight—which was feeling deliciously likely—like the current of a southern river. Slowly he retrieved the bits and pieces that were left of his life: a chicken split in two, not precisely for the purpose of making a sandwich, a home lost for ever (since dignity is deeper than poverty), an inept partner who had been his entire misfortune, and the gala costume hired from the Artists' Boutique, all sweaty, white, tattered. Perhaps where he was now was his natural place in the world. Perhaps this was the last resting place fate had ordained for his bones. He saw the Beast scratching at the ground and thought that just a shallow cleft in the garbage heap would be enough for his own body. There, under the earth, a redeeming dream would come and he would be carried away within it as in a dark tram, and when the snouts of dogs and rats came to look for him he would be far away, dissolved finally into his images.

His partner put the cock's body into the hole, then took its head out of his handkerchief and placed it precisely above the neck, as if completing a jigsaw. Then he built up a little mound of earth over the body, and finished by smoothing it over with his palms. With his middle finger he drew a cross, sighed, and pressed his hands into a scrap of newspaper as if it were a towel. Señor Pequeño scrutinized the sky, empty of clouds, breeze or birds, and said to himself that the world was infinite indifference. He said to himself that his life was like a chalk drawing on a school blackboard which the children wipe away and forget and that just as nobody asks where the clouds go as they pass by and disappear so the footballer had hit the mark when he had predicted for him the true significance of his exit from the stage. Furthermore, Señor Pequeño said to himself that what he was currently doing was thinking. He said to himself that this was something he had never done before. And he said to himself as well that he understood why. That he understood that to think was to link together a long chain of indifference. Like he who joined together the sky and the earth, the sea and the seagulls, men and volcanoes, and the night and the stars. He saw the suitcase with his professional props and thought that these materials of entertainment were refuse, knives without edge, hammers without heads, mouths without tongues. When the Beast got up to peer out of their hiding place, yawning big like a mountain, it was sufficient to see his face to know that they had been discovered.

"Run, Dad!" he shouted.

"You're a fool as big as yourself!" said Señor Pequeño, without abandoning his position in the dirt. "What infinite misfortune!"

The swindled punters fell on them without words, wet with perspiration and panting. Three of them went for the Beast while the other decided he'd be enough on his own for the little man. They left nothing unbeaten, neither thighs, nor kidneys, nor chest, nor noses. The Beast tried to cover himself with the prop suitcase, but when they took him from behind he had to let it go, feeling one of them stabbing him with an intricately wrought doorkey, while the others dealt him meticulous punches, one after another, with the precision of a sewing machine. The cock fighter who was taking care of Señor Lecaros soon gave up beating him, surprised at meeting no resistance. Two kicks in the stomach were enough to leave the little man inert. So he turned him face downwards and dragged him over to a mud-hole to humiliate him in the face. When both of them were still, their attackers piled them on top of each other and cleaned themselves on the sleeves of their shirts, satisfied with such rapid vengeance but fearful that they might have left too many marks. They returned to the street walking unhurriedly, but not exactly slowly.

It took an hour for the Beast to wake up, and a few minutes more to separate the coagulated eyelashes of his right eye. At his first movement he had the sensation that the earth was a kind of ship and that the tongue inside his split mouth had the texture of milk. Some parts of his body were insensible, and he supported himself on these, as those he could feel were assailed by burning and stinging. He confirmed that his partner was still alive and, removing his white jacket, folded it beneath the back of his head, positioning himself beside him so that his huge shadow would prevent the sun advancing over Señor Pequeño's face. Then he set about scraping off the clots of mud until Señor Pequeño himself raised a diminutive hand to shade his nose and eyes, saying to him in an infinitely distant voice:

"Leave me alone."

At which the Beast leaned his own head on the ground, while the dream brought darkness over Señor Pequeño's body inch by inch, like someone departing a house at night.

The policeman witnesses what Señor Pequeño has just suffered and the water from a hydrant falls on the ochre slash of the scar on his head. The sun shines on the waste-ground and begins to strike blinding flashes from stones and cobbles. Scattered about are masks, conical magicians' hats, melted records by Al Jolson and Bunny Berrigan, false cottonwool paunches, masters of ceremonies' batons. The policeman circles round them in a silence which crackles, as if a bush were burning in the distance. He approaches Señor Pequeño and says, "Is that you?" He tilts his head and adds, "I nearly didn't recognise you with your face like that." He studies the heavens as if sniffing on-coming rain and with his hands behind his back asks: "Laid about you, did they?" He knocks with his foot against the golden case. He murmurs, "Things?" He takes out a green handkerchief made of the cloth used to cover gaming tables and wipes the sweat from his forehead. "Best if you come along with me." The Beast and he get up and walk behind the constable in a yellowish gloom. "Now then, you two," says the policeman. "Want an apple?"

Taking out three from his pouch he distributes them around with solemn equity. He encourages the partners to tuck in. He says: "I like to hear the sound they make. If you eat them quickly, I'll show you a photograph. We go this way." Señor Pequeño says: "There's a country that's made up of birds with very soft plumage of colours that nobody has seen. It's a country that expands and contracts as the birds sleep or fly. The country reaches as far as the furthest bird can fly and stops where that bird can touch wings with another bird. In that country there is nothing other than birds and air." The policeman says: "How do you know?" and "Eat your apple". Señor Pequeño chews the fruit: "My Mother and Father took off on a balloon flight around 1940. Beforehand we took some photos in the fairground and they dressed like a bride and bridegroom. The balloon had no motor, and for every kiss between the bridal couple it rose a few yards until they wound their tongues together, and it never stopped again. I think my parents are in the country of the birds." The Beast asks if they are hot. "It's desperately hot," opines the policeman. The Beast, all dressed in white, wants to know if they need him to wet them. Señor Pequeño and the policeman agree it would be a blessing if it would rain. The Beast presses his chest and from his arms spurts water which envelopes them like an automatic irrigator and the Beast's smile is the sluice which releases or shuts off the flow. "That's enough, man," says the constable. "Turn off that tempest before it ruins my photo." Señor Pequeño and the Beast need to know which photo that is. The policeman says that's fine. He kneels on the ground and exhibits a poster, after first smoothing it out with the palms of his hands, and there is a face on it which Señor Lecaros admits is familiar. "Count to three," says the policeman, "and we'll see if you can tell me his name." Señor Pequeño replies: "That man is the Commissioner." "A grand person," murmurs the constable, folding the poster as it was before. "It's a portrait I don't show to many because the rain wets it the sun burns it the wind rends it the snow freezes it." He adds: "It's my very favourite song, which says I dreamt the snow was burning I dreamt the fire froze over." "Strange," says Señor Pequeño, "Maybe I once sang that song in a circular theatre lined with blue velvet." "Life is full of misfortune and coincidence," argued the constable, "without which we would be as cold and as distant as all those planets revolving up there without knowing why."

They are sitting in the reception hall, which is full of violinists, magicians, clowns, *bolero* singers, rubber men. They wait while the assistant notes down their personal details, and their faces break into colours according to the fall of light filtering on to them through the stained-glass windows. When the stenographer approaches, the constable says straight into his ear: "They're here recommended by the Commissioner". The stenographer brandishes his notebook. "What entertainments can you provide?" Says the Beast, permitting the stenographer to insert his head into his bag: "I play this." Says Señor Pequeño: "Impressions, American tap, general master of ceremonies." The stenographer walks to the cupboad. He opens the door. He makes them come over. Hung there are gala costumes, Greek tunics, pumpkins with holes, streamers, birthday bonnets, monkey masks, monster outfits, toothy masks, frankenstein, dracula, batman and penguin suits, crowns, first communion dresses, rapiers, carnival tricks, Christmas trees, Markman toy train tracks, maps of the world, fairy costumes, masks. Now Señor Pequeño is sporting patent leather shoes with white pom-poms, a waisted smoking jacket and a red bowler. Abundant on the Beast's head is a red wig, beneath it a white tunic of worked gauze and on his shoulders a frame from which rose and fell wings made of metal, elastic and cardboard when a plastic string was pulled. "You look terrific," says the constable. The stenographer leads them through a gallery of blue moss which gives onto the stage. Behind the scenery there are cardboard trees and cows cut out with carpenter's scissors. At the far end, however, the rocks and ocean are

157

precise and tangible. A wind begins to blow and Señor Pequeño advances towards the dais holding down his bowler with his hand, while the Beast's tunic flaps in the breeze as in a Viking embarkation. The impresario appears, followed by the stenographer, and they take up position immediately below the prompt box, in an armchair of ochre velvet and a Viennese chair. The impresario claps his hands and the act begins. The Beast pulls out the trumpet from his breast and Señor Pequeño says: "What's that for?" "An ignoble acquisition." "You are my shame," remarks Señor Pequeño. The Beast lifts the mouthpiece to his lips and emits a pristine sound, which ebbs and circles in space as if braiding the air. The impresario beats his baton and cries, his voice confused with the tide: "What was that noise?" Furious, he comes forward, hardly able to support the curve of his spine, and beats his baton on the edge of the stage until it shivers into splinters. The stenographer hands him another, and the impresario points at the two of them above while the clouds move in counter-direction to the sea, as swift as aeroplanes. "This is bad business!" he complains. "Your laziness demeans the art of the show. All the time there are fewer mothers interested in celebrating their children's birthdays. There are few enough birthdays anyway, and I control them all. They have come here to see just the act they need, and you conduct yourselves like drugged mules. If you please, do me the favour of beginning with what you know, as at any moment my coronary may become stimulated and I'll be off to the land of beyond! Were you responsible for that noise?" "Begging your pardon, sir," says the Beast self-abasingly. "Not to worry, son. I enjoyed the noise." "A musical number," announces Señor Pequeño. The impresario is getting angry again: "When I want a tale, I read a story book. I don't need you to tell me anything. Just get on with it. Mediocre artists you may be, but at least have pity on my coronary. Do the noise again. It was a good start." Señor Pequeño goes over to the gramophone and sets the needle down on a record of Ted Wyms with his whistle and orchestra playing "Whispering". He tap dances on the boards, his face rigid though his feet leap and whirl, and where the drums beat one measure Señor Pequeño fits in four. The Beast tries to imitate him but the wind and his trunklike skeleton make him totter and sway like an unfortunate doll putting up with the blows of the children at the market. The impresario cries out: "Brilliant! Brilliant!" And adds: "Pull the string now! Move the wings, move the wings!" "The wings," repeats the Beast, and stops his movements in order to operate the mechanism. The impresario twists his legs, on the edge of releasing a flow of urine. "You're out to be the accomplice in my murder. Move the wings but don't stop dancing, stupid chicken!" Señor Pequeño, who has stopped his routine, stares at him with his tongue hanging out of his mouth. "Keep on dancing, you! What kind of indiscipline is this? And you, keep on playing! Come on! Cooooome ooooon!" The Beast pulls at the plastic cord. His feet take off from the stage and he hangs half a yard in the air. The impresario takes the handkerchief proffered by his stenographer and wipes his face, overcome with emotion. "It worked," he cries. "Now what are you doing, stupid, stuck up there like a traffic light? Come down." The Beast jerks the cord and returns to earth. "What kind of artists are you? Why have you stopped playing? Morons!" He lifts his hand to his throat and tries to dislodge a kind of knot which is suffocating him. The stenographer plunges his hands around his neck and presses from behind. At which the impresario says: "It's all right. I'm better now. Next time try not to massacre my jugular." He adjusts his tie and offers them the most cordial of hands: "My warmest congratulations! You're on. Next Sunday you'll perform at a birthday at this address. You're on the payroll." In the moonlight, Señor Pequeño, the constable and the Beast read the card. "We did it, Dad?" Señor Pequeño snaps: "You shut up! From now on I work only with professionals." "But, Dad, they've signed us up!" "I don't care!" The constable says: "You can't betray the Commissioner. A thief's fate awaits you, nicking chickens here and there." "I'm getting out of this city," says Señor Pequeño. "Everyone here wants to destroy me. I'll catch a bus before I change my mind." The constable lowers his head and puts his hands together as if praying in church. "They pushed my face in the mud like a frog." He turns towards the Beast and says to him, before setting off for the beach: "The partnership we swore is dissolved." "What'll I do without you, Dad?" says his partner, following him and trying to take from him the bag of variety costumes which Señor Pequeño is carrying listlessly. Señor Pequeño extricates himself from this attempt, and points at the plastic cord in the middle of his chest. "Pull on that string and fly away." He lets him take the case, and looks him up and down: "You look ridiculous in that get-up," he manages to tell him.

I'll come with you Fats, and Fats you'll get bored, and Arturo I'll get more bored here, by now I know the stains on the ceiling by heart, and Fats it's just that you won't enjoy it, and never mind, just out of curiosity, then. And they went together to the factory out of curiosity. But there's no time wasted with Fats and when the treasurer's report was over and the welfare report he just slipped things in in that way Fats has of slipping things in when he's got something on his mind, letting things come from the people themselves, raising the issue so that the blokes discover it for themselves, not saying the words himself but forming them in the others' mouths through questions and silences. That's why Fats is their representative, because they all want what he wants and what they want Fats never forces on them, and so Fats let slip how are the recreational activities going, *compañeros*, and now about the testimonial theatre, and above all *compañeros* what about the sports arrangements, and El Negro who's as sharp as a tack when it comes to intuition, really, *compañeros* this sports thing does affect the factory 'cos it'd be a fine thing for all these great lumps here to give up being spectator-sportsmen and there are guts on some around here that are frightening, *compañeros*, and Skinny who was squeezing his fingers said they'd found a pitch, but the lads' playing was all over the shop, they were worse than those jerks in the National Team, and there was no pleasure in it when ten minutes after the *compañeros* got stuck in of a Sunday their tongues were hanging out as if they were

161

wiping down the field, and, sure, afterwards they were stars when it came to knocking back the booze and wrapping their tongues around the chicken bones in the *cazuela*, and with athletes like that it's not worth the candle sacrificing yourself to achieve anything, and the boys and others aah, put it up Skins don't exaggerate, remember the match against Municipales and the other against Hijos de Tarapaca, and Skinny come on let's be objective, *compañeros*, we won those matches for three simple reasons which you all know and which I don't want to repeat, go on, don't mind us Skins, what reasons were those, I said I'm not saying, yes you are, and Skinny very well seeing you insist we won against Municipales because they came on with only nine players and the ref threw off two more, against Hijos de Tarapaca because the *compañeritos* in defence laid into their kids in the forward line like a bunch of ultras and after the match the Tarapaca president made a *formal complaint, compañeros*, and the third reason, said Skinny almost tempted into grinning because everyone else was, the third reason is because God is Great and that's all *compañeros*, and come on now we're getting off the point here, let's hear what the *compañera* social visitor has to say, and Margarita raised her voice as soft as a dove and joking apart it's good that the recreational activity is getting off the ground once and for all because there are a lot of *compañeros* here who have a tendency to get soaked of a Saturday night and don't make it to voluntary work and a lot of wives who come and complain that the kids spend all day on the streets or wandering about half rickety or like ghosts because they go to the pool-rooms and never get a glimpse of the sun so joking apart let's see how we can keep up the recreational activity, and then Fats all casual, like the cardsharp who stays unimpressed even after the others have shown two pairs, three cards a full house and a royal flush, there's a *compañero* here with us who's a distinguished footballer, a true professional who's come to this meeting without any commitments but who maybe, who knows, maybe yes, maybe no, perhaps might be interested in training a factory team, in giving some classes on technique with the ball, who if he says no then it's no, no commitments, and then comes a short silence and then El Negro looks at Arturo, and Arturo looks around at the faces of all the *compañeros* and *compañeras*, and El Negro says the floor is yours to say what you feel *compañero* Arturo, if you think we should keep it up or whatever, and *señorita* Margarita waits all expectantly and Arturo imagines seeing her every day with those grey madonna's eyes and her nose a bit big on that soft face but big-nosed women are always gowers, good-'n-hot the darlin's, and he smiles at her, and she smiles at him, and Fats smiles, they're okay these kids thinks Arturo, they give me the time of day, they know I can be useful to them, they seem all right, and Arturo clears his throat and says that speaking personally he has a lot of training to get in, and there are certain people who are interested in him travelling abroad because there are some *gringos* who want to form a team which isn't just a bunch of savages, right, but after all, given the circumstances, and seeing as how there's a pitch ready, and seeing as how there's a changing-room ready, if there's anything he can do to help well sure, it's my pleasure, and if they want him to be trainer that's fine by him but on one condition and that is that there can only be one captain on any ship and if he's going to put in something then he'd hope that the *señores* will show some discipline because discipline is basic and if the call is at eight in the morning then the *señores* must be there at eight, and everyone, that's great, El Negro, tremendous, the *señora* social worker wonderful, at last, and Skinny it's great but please would *compañero* Arturo not call them *señores* but just *compañeros*, and Arturo grins and says well, I, but Fats gets in first and cuts him short and says these are details, life will decide whether it's *señor* or *compañero*, the game's the thing, not winning, and a whole load more cobblers which Fats comes out with, but everyone knows Fats is happy, and now we dish out the Orange Crush and same pâté sandwiches as ever and carry on chatting in groups, sorting out the details, a short break because now Fats has to go and coordinate arrangements in the industrial zone for the march on 4 September which really has to be a march to end all marches because the fascists want to show their claws but for all their claws they'll see out there just how many of us there are, just how many *compañeritos* there are at work in this country, and if one day they manage to win we'll see how long they can hang on, so I must be off, he said, and Arturo I'll come along with you for a bit, and Fats fine if you want to and endless handshakes all dirty with pâté sandwiches and *señorita* Margarita says she's going to come along on Sunday too, and Arturo "Really?" staring at her "Okay then" as if to say "I'll be waiting sweetheart", and she says yes, and she gets the message and comes over all coquette-like, yes, she'll be there it's a promise, and Fats and he go out into the street, and Fats is a bit ahead of him singing like the happy Fats he is, and it's night already and Fats makes a great job of that song by Raphael and Arturo feels a sensation of something good running up his spine, and he feels relaxed like coming in out of the cold, the relief of someone who finds his bed after feeling round his room in the dark, and he gives good ol' friendly tubby heart-of-gold Fats a punch and adds the second part to the Raphael song and Fats speeds up so as to get to the big textile factory where

164

the industrial contingent is to meet, and where they're walking more rapidly now is the darkest and roughest part, and the muddy holes are still soft from the drizzle last night, but Fats skirts them like a grasshopper, an athletic flea with radar senses, and moreover it's easier getting going because coming slowly up behind them in the road which runs lateral to the Gran Avenida is a car with its lights on, with its headlights lighting up the street, and Fats who hasn't realised what's happening says to Arturo bloody good luck that car behind because otherwise we'd have drowned in this bog by now, and Arturo thinks bloody good luck, and they don't see the two guys in helmets who are getting out of the car, or the five with their fingers wrapped in chains who are running silently behind while the one driving overtakes them and crosses in front of Fats and Arturo, and the others fall on them from behind like bats and carry Fats up against the wall and when they begin to beat him this is for being such a motherfucker and why don't you leave off fucking around in the union just so you know you don't mix it with our boys you fat queer the one left in the car revs up and the explosions of the motor eat up the cries and now he switches off the lights but in the glow of the moon filtering through the clouds Arturo sees Fats' mouth split by the chain and Arturo stands there as stiff as a post and now they're mashing Fats' ribs with their fists and burying their boots in his knees and very soon Fats is nothing but silence in the night and the one in the car punches the horn loudly but the others nothing they carry on dealing it out with their fists, with their fists they keep on at it, with the chain in his face, and Arturo still there, a billboard figure in the night, a soundless cry, a hand without a hand, a leg without a leg, a heart in suspension as if touched by frost, and eventually, finally, at last his body comes to life, one of the five stares at him good and long, looks at him like that and another of them also looks at him, and Fats' body slumps, and the ones who are staring at him approach with their chains held at cheek level and Arturo sees Fats' blood on the chain and now his body is alert as if receiving an electric shock from the cobbles and in a single bound he begins running towards the lamp-lit street, there where the factory spurts out the smoke from the labours of other workes like Fats, and runs without stopping, and runs without looking back any more, and runs even more when the car begins to move forward, and now he can feel the car half a block from him, the car yards from him, inches from him, and then he thinks now it's coming it's all up and a hand from the window encourages him with a blow to the back of his neck, and he trips, and picks himself up before hitting the ground and sets off running again and those in the car hem him in against the wall as if to butt against him, as if they were the horse and he the cow in a rodeo, and that's how his body feels, awkward, without strength, like a cow, exactly like a cow, and now it's just the two of them the horse and him scraping along the wall inches between them and he senses the laughter of the five, the five who are now blowing the horn at full blast and beating the chains against the sides of the car to terrify the cow, stifling it in the narrow strip separating it from being crushed, and then one of them sticks out his head and shouts what are you running for, arsehole, what are you all bunched up there for, shitbag, and he can just make out the face of the one who overtaking him now shouts what are you running for, bastard, what's so important about you, little fucker, and then the car disappears round the corner and Arturo carries on running away, as if now he was pursuing them, except that it's not like that, and Arturo begins to scream out sons-of-bitches

over and over again, and pants and doesn't stop running, and doesn't stop shouting, and his mouth says
sons-of-bitches over and over again, and then just
son-of-a-bitch, son-of-a-bitch it says son-of-a-bitch it
says again son-of-a-bitch and now it's no longer heat
that he has on his cheeks but sweat, fierce, salty, endless, and there he is running and by now he doesn't
know why he's running nor that while he's saying
son-of-a-bitch, while he shouts it over and over again
he's thinking of Fats' silence, of Fats' mouth and the
chain, doesn't know that when he shouts and shouts
he's thinking of a person who is so close to him it is
him, right there with him, a person who is him,
Arturo, yes Arturo in person, himself, and sure, when
Fats had slumped down he had looked at him, Osorio's
mouth was open as if saying *Arturo* and maybe he
hadn't said it because in his heart Fats had always
known that this wasn't a word to keep inside yourself, and if that word wasn't in Fats' heart then much
less would it appear on that rough tongue, much less
now that that pink tongue was impregnated with
scarlet blood from the pierced cheek, and sure now he
could see it there, damnably there, Fats' mouth open
in a shape which could be Arturo, or help me, or reach
out to me hold me love me, or rescue me, or save me,
or more likely it was a final sound which Fats had
transmitted in a magic circuit, inaccessible, when his
face had laughed at himself, at his own pain, when his
mouth split by the blow of the chain had had time for
that smile, so that Arturo would bear it with him
through the city night, that final sound of son-of-a-
bitch which once again was making him run, now no
longer through the industrial emptiness with its
chimneys and furnaces of the machines, but here in
the city centre itself, colliding with peaceful couples,
the sweet violet sellers, the cars, the postboxes, the
billboards, and always with the back of his neck

throbbing faster than he could make his legs work, or than the single, persistent, final whistle over which passed the tape with the same four words, that rhythm with which his own face fell to pieces in a splintered mirror, in the shameless shopwindows which reflected back his image among dummies, shoes going cheap, multicoloured cloth, between light textured bodices and linen goods, and the more he ran, the four words became flesh of his body, breath of his panting, bites of his teeth, the cry on his tongue, and now he could hardly run any further, and yet he could, now he almost preferred to die, but he still ran, and on he ran like that, swollen, suffocated: alive.

over to you then, Facus, tell me how you see the action so far, poised over it like a wild beast lying in wait for its prey, mouth hot, watchful falcon's eyes infinitely, millimetrically alert

many thanks, Marquez, for your overflowing generosity in employing epithets of which I am unworthy as I'm no more than a human being who has the joy of being able to serve our listeners through my humble eyes which are as fallible as any others and at times more so due to the professional incapacities caused by their irritated pupils being worn out by the flirtatious dance of the ball

very well said, Facus, I've always been of the opinion that what your eyes miss your tongue sees, that eloquence which is worth a ton of good Spanish in its exaltation of the encomiastic arts of our national gamesmen

Thank you, Marquez, as far as I'm concerned, given that anything you say is law, and without going any further, if you'll forgive this emotional outburst, I'm reminded of that biblical phrase so widely diffused in our schools where future patriots are being formed, I'm referring to that phrase which goes 'in the beginning was the word', I imagine that God must have been thinking of that word when your good parents brought you, via the stork, into this world

well, Facus, I feel you're exaggerating, a professional of language such as I is set neither below nor above other mortals and precisely what you have just quoted should be the motto that guides our conduct as narrators of events; not feeling privileged because effort or chance ordained that this magic apparatus called a microphone should have fallen into our nervous hands to bring joy, culture and entertainment to thousands of listeners, and now, Facus, if it's not indiscreet, what did you think of that move, in your view was it a penalty?

listen, Marquez, a penalty as such it wasn't because the referee didn't order one, and if the referee didn't call it then unless by some miraculous art the world were turned backwards like a gigantic grinding machine in space which pulls things back to their points of origin, that violation can never now be called by anyone, so Flecha fans will have to carry it in their hearts like an abortion or a dark black crow pecking at their most sensitive organs, so any discussion about whether it was a penalty or wasn't a penalty would be a mere gallimaufry, Marquez, byzantine, and we can't have that

quite right, Facus, quite right, nevertheless for our listeners' information how did the incident appear to you?

well, Marquez, for the sake of shedding light on the matter and for the record of this championship I'll give you my judgement: penalty, Marquez, penalty that's all there is to it! Garcia made a short pass down the inside edge of the field near the corner flag looking for Santillana, who returned sideways to Garcia, which allowed the player, as he opened up, to see Arturo's frenetic entry from the centre of the pitch, and shoot level towards the centre, way forward, as if he'd set his kick by the compass, to the precise point on home territory where Arturo was to arrive; so the Flecha star made contact with the ball, bringing it to earth with a blow of his boot which to many sounded like a corpse being thrown into a grave, eliminated the threat of Navarro with a dribbling manoeuvre, and upon confronting the goalkeeper, man to man alone, the latter hurled himself not at the ball, but straight at Arturo's legs preventing him from moving his lower extremities freely and thus from turning into reality what nestled in the hearts of the fans neither as intimation nor intuition but as certainty that the ball was about to go to the very back of the net and, naturally, as this was not to be its destiny, the fans experienced first the ravages of anger and immediately then the bitter undertow of desperation, do you follow, Marquez?

I follow, and as always, from my commentator's box on high, am with you, Facus, however far from home base your mission as a journalist may take you, and was just about to say to you myself that with respect to the manoeuvre in question I received a similar impression, that is to say that the goalkeeper annulled the mobile capacity of the lower Arturian limbs with the malintentioned vigour of someone who is no longer content just to defend, wouldn't you say?

yes, Marquez

but more than to defend to paralyse, bury, grind his opponent into the turf rather than let him achieve his destiny of a goal, Facus

exactly, Marquez, exactly, there was the first fragrance of a goal in that move, and rapidly that aroma which a fan's discriminating nose recognises when his skin tingles and his body seethes on the terrace, became the penetrating perfume of a super-goal because the entire galaxy saw that *that* was a penalty, the entire galaxy apart from the ref; I respect the gentlemen in black and short pants even though they are often treated like vultures of evil omen, but it is a fact, Marquez, that the Football Association does at times make available to rival teams gents in black who appear to be dressed like that as a kind of visiting card indicating utterly clouded brains, and please don't see in that remark any racist allusion nor any discourtesy towards the splendid black race

black is beautiful, Facus!

yes it is, Marquez

after all, I, less than anyone, with my considerably sunburned complexion, have any right to let slip a single anti-democratic word and you can testify to my spirit as a man of libertarian ideas, Facus

I so testify, Marquez, here, on the pitch, before an attorney, or in church before God if necessary

I thank you and continue, Facus, as I was saying among these gents in black who frequently distort the inherent spirit of the game with their inopportune whistles there are many who suffer from serious visual difficulties, Facus, advanced cases of astigmatism and cataracts; I've seen some of them in the privacy of their own homes using glasses for something as simple as observing the television from a distance of no more than a yard; without mentioning others who long since left behind the gym and the *mens sana* on the bar cardtable among full houses and royal flushes and pairs, and leaving aside altogether the Sunday lunches which many of them swallow down before epiphanizing on the pitch to direct the match, true bacchanalia of good pasta, excellent ravioli, superb sauce, fine cheeses and, why not spell it out

clearly, the marvellous wines which have always cha-
racterized this land, none of which would have any
importance on the spectators' benches, let's say, or
for commentators like us who make more use of our
tongues than our legs, and if you'll excuse the figure
of speech without imagining that there's any allusion intended to your slight paunch, Facus

no offense, Marquez, those in glass houses, you
know, Marquez, nor can the pot call the kettle

but to call things by the names used on the terraces,
if you have to move from here to there following the
sallies, feints and dance of the ball, it does matter if
you're weighed down by a belly, and when that black
speck is left cut off from the action and the move
ends up in a penalty which was seen by the whole stadium, and how I'd like to have an action replay here
so that the amateurs won't doubt my word, the natural
anger of the crowd is aroused and the players', and
then the heads start to get hot and then hands and,
well, you know how these to-do's end up

in effect, Marquez, they end up like this one ended
up, to parody that verse by the poet Parra where he
says "the party was good, it lasted until it ended"

exactly, Facus, exactly, and among other things, if
anything came to an end here it was Arturo's reputation, always so long as you don't see in my words any
conclusive and negative judgement regarding the
young Flecha star, because I have the impression
that his expulsion from the turf occurred just as he
was putting the final touches to his first great ingeni-
ous move in a match which at that time was thirty
minutes into its second half

apropos, Marquez, we're now thirty eight minutes
into the second half and Flecha are attacking. Lux,
for youthful skin!

thank you, Facus, I repeat that if we were to pile
the eighty minutes of play onto one side of the scales

and on the other the dross of mistakes committed and opportunities squandered by Arturo, the scales would murmur, supposing it was one of those speak-your-weight machines in Diana's Entertainments, the scales would murmur gravely in their operatic baritone: nothing, demonstrating in its vertical tension its verdict on the actions of him who was a star but is one no longer, who can never again be a star except in that very moment of glory which justly earned him his being sent off, I don't know, Facus, how you saw that sequence of events which led referee Molina to take the drastic step of pulling up and censuring Arturo with the red card, and I assure you that I and all your listeners await your version of the facts so that it may be recorded in the book of definitive and unappealable judgements

thank you, Marquez, thank you *señores* listeners, for such unlimited trust, I can only say with all my heart that your confidence moves me so deeply that I can do no more than respond with a truthful, brief and exact synthesis of the unhappy facts which culminated in Arturo's being sent off; a confused incident took place in the region of the corner flag from which Garcia emerged in possession then touched short to a teammate, receiving the ball straight back again, and then estimating the lightning speed at which Arturo was burning down from the very centre of the pitch like a comet blazing its trail across the green heavens of the turf, Garcia delivered the ball to him at an obtuse angle of some twenty degrees, and as ball and Arturo's boot now clung together in secret adultery both sporting items moved forward together and when the goal-bells were already sounding in those lovely cathedrals of the fans' hearts goal-keeper Pizzuti took possession of both Arturo's legs with the evident purpose of obstructing his transla-tion forwards; as a result of this incident, and as a natural physical consequence, Arturo's body was precipitated towards the ground, and the sound "penalty" came together in its three syllables in mouths throughout the stadium at which the player sat on the ground condemned to await the sanctioning whistle, while the spectators sought out the sombre shadow of referee Molina in the large expanse of the other team's half, we commentators and professionals of the microphone waiting for the finger of the referee to signal pointedly from the other end of the pitch towards the critical location at the end of twelve regulation paces (and it would be true to say that everyone, even Pizzuti himself, was beginning to crouch down between the three poles which like the three masts of a caravel floated in the unfading blue sky of this Latin American homeland) when something happened which no one suspected: the referee waved his right hand in front of his face, not exactly to fan himself, but to indicate with that traditional gesture *no, nothing doing, gentlemen*, but, Marquez, facts have an irreversible mechanism and what happened *happened* and the whole stadium saw it; however much room for subjectivism football may allow there are certain moral coordinates which must not be violated if the very integrity of the spectacle is to be maintained; here, the referee, like a tiny black insect, like a diminutive David hurling from the catapult of his authority the pebble of an error at the face of that many-faced Goliath which is the national public, the most gentlemanly in the Americas, broke the limits of all prudence, and so how can one not justify, although it has no justification, that Arturito, wounded on this day of low grey clouds, should get up from his position on the turf, upbraid him with his fist and then finally convey the latter with singular violence towards the referee's jaw, laying him out instantaneously, what do you say, Marquez?

I say that's right, Facus, that that's exactly how things were, and by my watch we're now forty-five minutes into the second half and the game will be stopped at any moment with Flecha down by one goal to nil, Miquel's goal after fifteen minutes of the first half, and the ever-moving hands of the clock are looking to make reputations at exactly forty-five minutes, and it's all nearly over, *señores*, with just the last few agonising seconds to live through, and before these microphones are discharged of the precious energy which feeds them and together with the noble players we set off for a well-deserved rest I'd like to hear your valuable final summary of the game, away we go, Facus

well, Marquez, the conclusion to be drawn from this match can be summed up in three simple words: *same as always*, another fever of high hopes produced in the lower divisions by a prodigy which, if you'll permit the metaphor, snaps on his second outing onto the pitch like a fragile branch in autumn; an attempt to impress all and sundry sailing on the tempestuous ocean of the poor clubs, but which finishes up with a reputation accumulated in the hold lost in the cold salt sea where no fine fruit can grow; we came to see the launch of a rocket to fame and what we witnessed was the shipwreck of a row boat, because Arturo's performance can merit no other judgement from the experts; lazy in its take-off, unprepared when it came to retaking defensive positions, tangled up in fancy dribbling while the wings were waiting for long passes, in short, all the typical ills and endemic evils of our Latin American talents which augur disaster in the World Cup in Germany for the chances of a continent which once upon a time was the cradle of Pele, Labruna and the immortal Tucho Mendez, whom Armando Bo put onto the silver screen in his deeply felt *Ball of Rags*, in short, it's high time the lads who debate with the ball and the trainers who coach them woke up to the fact that it's all very well to be trained in building castles in the air and lighting up the night with firework displays, but they should realise that the castles collapse and the fireworks fade away in the night of passing time leaving joy among the naive, to be sure, but no real foundations for an edifice which could give this Latin America, so much loved and so much our own, as many soccer stars as those which shine in its young sky, what do you say, Marquez

that's it, Facus, that's it, I add my signature to what you have written, you have been generous and God willing Flecha's ambitions will lead to a good end and what happened this evening will be no more than a gaffe, a nightmare at the edge of a dream, a grease stain on the albion shirt of the sport and that next Sunday they will have fully recovered, and that Arturo remembers once and for all, now that his punishment has been dished out and taken on board, that he was the spermatozoa that engendered so many hopes in his club and, why not be honest about it, in you and I, who are nobody but who a month ago placed in him the hopes which seemed appropriate; now back to the studio for our signature tune

"Señora, is Susana in?"

That's how he said it. But for minutes beforehand he'd been hovering in the shadows near the doorbell before pressing it. It had been as insufferable for him to go away from the house as to approach it, and furthermore he hadn't showered after the game and now his body shared the same dampness as the shirt in his blue canvas bag.

"Who wants her?"

Another name another face another body another calling. He'd have to say Arturo after which the woman's thin lips would part like a stork's beak to smile: "I'll go and see if she's in".

"A friend," he said. The mother's mouth stood out sharp with its tiny teeth and she almost watched him with that mouth, studied his confusion with that mouth. "Arturo," he gave in.

"Just a moment."

He heard the steps die away in the shadows and imagined the conversation between mother and daughter in the confidential intimacy of the room. Mothers always think those ringing at the door are a bunch of hymen-savaging degenerates and look at their daughters' boyfriends as if to say, "You'll do no such dirty things to my little girl".

"She wants to know what you want."

Had she been waiting the whole afternoon for the fly to land on the grain of sugar and was this to be the sublime moment in which her hand would flatten it?

"That if it's all right, *señora*, I'd like to speak to her personally."

"And what might it be about?"

"Tell her..."—he pretended he had something in his eye—"tell her it's about *compañero* Osorio."

"Are you from the Party?"

"No, *señora*."

"I'll tell her, all right?"

Now he was afraid that she herself, Susana, would appear at the door to skewer him with her "What d'you want?", categorical, dark, desirable, but someone else's, meant for someone else. For seconds he soaked up the sweat on his forehead and temples with the canvas bag.

"She says come in."

She led him into the living room and indicated the armchair where he should sit. Arturo looked over the family portraits, the view of the *cordillera*-always-present-in-my-heart, the president's photo, this time with the first lady, the ballerinas, the family group in some amusement park around the 1940s, and that girl with the fine, fresh mouth was Susana's mother and she was as content as all women when they have their photos taken with their husbands in restaurants or amusement parks. Just at that moment he'd have liked to light a cigarette, but there weren't any either in his jacket or on the table.

Susana arrived with her hand outstretched and a polite smile. Although it wasn't what he was feeling like doing, Arturo stood up like a gentleman and exchanged a handshake. She sat down on the arm of the chair and now the same hand he'd shaken offered him a packet of cigarettes. He took one, and put it in his mouth, while the girl offered him the lighter before his hand could leave the edge of the seat. He'd picked up the next gesture from the films, where you look into the girl's eyes as she lights your cigarette, and so he did. But she looked at the flame and withdrew her fingers as his draw made the end glow brighter. He noticed she wasn't half as pretty as at other times, and her hair, without the restraints of ribbons and fringes, made her cheeks look a little puffy although maybe, he thought, that's because she's been asleep.

"Okay, then, what d'you want?" she said, after returning to the chair.

"Have you seen Osorio?"

"Why?"

"How is he?"

"He's got a bullet in his shoulder—did you know?"

"A bullet?"

He watched the cigarette burning down and suddenly took a deep drag. He held back the smoke, staring at the floor.

"Did he say anything about me?"

"What d'you mean?"

"Something, anything?"

"Like what?"

He thought the girl knew, that she knew completely and absolutely everything, and had the place, the time and what had happened at her fingertips, but had prepared a luxurious revenge, and wanted him, Arturo, that little bastard Arturo, to come out with it all himself, with her as if butter wouldn't melt in her mouth. He looked up, expecting to meet the tricky gaze of a hip chick used to wrapping guys round her little finger. But the eyes were Susana's, the same as always, a little sleepier maybe, a little less spirited, but detached, calmly curious. Arturo swallowed. His free hand moved to squeeze her wrist, and she managed to pull away in time.

"I was with him last night. Didn't he tell you?"

"No."

"I was with him when they got him."

"You were there?"

"Yes."

"And?"

"And what?"

"What did you do?"

Arturo buried his nails in his knees.

"Nothing," he said.

For a long time Susana tidied her hair, sorting out its waves, then looked at him and shrugged her shoulders.

"I don't get you," she said. "They took Fats, you were there, and you couldn't do anything. Did they grab you too?"

"No. I stood there like a lemon, watching."

"While they were beating up Fats?"

"And then I split."

Susana began to blink without pausing, as if faced with a difficult calculation and the pulse of her brain was disturbing her eyes.

"You took off like a creep?" she said softly, almost cautiously, as if afraid of offending him, almost, almost sure the reply would be, "no, it wasn't like that, you haven't understood".

Arturo felt this was much worse than last night. Last night he'd simply been a creep, and had lost his home, his friends, even his magic with the ball. But now all that was left of him was the image of a scared rabbit fleeing from an ambush. He felt sterile, convinced that no good milk would ever flow from his belly, that his seed would be indifferent dust wherever he sowed it, because from it could flow nothing but himself, tepid, viscous, useless. He abominated himself down to his last wile, the spoiled child seeking forgiveness through sweetness, for being on the point of dissolving into tears in front of her because he didn't have the balls to go to the hospital to see Fats' open mouth, his mouth split by the bleeding chain wound, the man with the bullet in him. He had turned to Susana pretending that this she-militant, this carnal sister to Fats, this girl in her headband and scarlet blouse, her miner's helmet and shirt knotted at the belly-button painting revolutionary murals, was a little raven-like priest at confession to whom he could sell treachery for absolution, masturbation for liturgy, a little breast-beating to cover his betrayal. He felt that here he had reached the end of his journey. That he had crossed the desert in search of the city and had not found it. That there was nothing more than himself. That the waters of the oasis were neither magic, nor holy, nor held within their depths mysterious sunken cities with cordial and sportive ladies and princes.

He began to weep, there on the edge of the chair, tears which at first were his own softness spilling from his eyes, his own cold semen, his breath, until the waters shook him like a storm and his whole body was a flood and his sobs broke the silence, turned over the table, and lifted him, blinded, his hands to his face, fused in the water with the ballerinas, the fine veins on Susana's neck, the yellowing curtains, the vase with its shaking flowers, and Susana's mother deploying her sharp mouth and immense eyes in the room now, and he wailing, hoarse, animal, like a bad actor who weeps when his lines have run out.

The girl took him by the elbow and guided him down the narrow passageway towards her room. She sat him on her bed and held his wrists, while he worked his head from side to side, gushing onto the quilt and onto the floor, as weak as a dying man. The older woman put her head round the door.

"What's the matter, young man? Are you ill?"

Susana pushed her gently out.

"Go away, Mother."

The woman pointed to Arturo with her chin.

"You know I don't like you taking visitors to your bedroom, dear."

The girl closed the door. She could sense her mother

was still there spying, and spoke through the wood.

"Please, Mother, leave us alone."

There was a scratching of the woman's nails at the door.

"Shall I bring him a glass of water? A little brandy?"

"It's all right, Mother. Just go away, please."

She went over to the bed and with the sleeve of her flower-patterned blouse began to wipe his sobbing cheeks, lips and neck.

"I only came to blubber all over your bed," stammered the youth, attempting a smile which only set off a second spasm despite his efforts to control it with his fists in his eyes.

"Lie down," she ordered. "Take off your shoes and lie down."

The youth undid the laces, obeying like a doll the instructions of a ventriloquist. The girl locked the door, waited for Arturo to lie down and covered him with the quilt.

"Stay there 'til I get back."

When Susana returned, Arturo had turned over on the bed and let his last tears flow down the cheek which was pressed against the wall. The girl approached him with a glass of water. She put it into his hands. Arturo propped himself up on his elbows and, before drinking, wet his fingers in the liquid and wiped his eyelids.

"Am I a real mess?" he said.

"Your eyes are like meat pies. Drink the water." When he had finished it, he rolled the glass on his cheeks, then gave it back to Susana with an attempt at a smile. "What's to be done with you?"

"Not much, it looks like."

"Looks like."

The young man combed through his hair with his fingers.

"Sorry about the crying and all that. It's the first time it's happened to me. Dunno what your old lady must think."

"Doesn't matter. How d'you feel now?"

Arturo worked up the courage to look her in the eyes, and saw his own image dilating in the pupils.

"Don't ask me that, or I'll start all over again."

"In a bad way?"

At that moment the lad knew he could weep the whole world out, as if his tears were held back behind the wall of his nose as complete and full as ever. He felt as if he were made of a single grief, longer and more attached to him than his shadow, and that when his tears were drained, the grief would continue, his own, intimate. But at the same time that shitty grief had something warm about it which sheltered him. He felt contained within his grief as if curled in a belly, inside a room where all his favourite things were tidily arranged and bathed in the softest of lights. He knew that this grief was truly his, made to measure, with his same chestnut eyes, and that it didn't end where his skin held in all his shame, but was a grief which also had tentacles, its own eyes, and another skin which covered his flesh and made it better. He wanted to tell Susana this, he wanted to tell her, that he didn't know what it was, that now he had something, that now it was as if he was in love with his own grief. But for Arturo none of this came as words. He put out his arm and drew the girl's fingernails gently towards him. He kissed and caressed them with his lips at the same time. First he let his saliva say I love you, let the new softness which his skin of grief was weaving into his flesh say it, let his breast, suddenly deeper, say it. Then he said the words.

"D'you know I love you?"

The girl had let his hair fall onto her shoulder. He

held her shoulder and in his fingers felt his grief once again. Susana didn't look at him.

"I'm sorry, Arturo," she said, softly and without drawing away, "you know I don't love you."

"Not a little?"

"Today, a little," smiled the girl.

"I wanted to tell you something, but I don't know how. It's like a hurt I feel, know what I mean?"

Susana passed her hand over his neck and made him raise his face. For a minute she looked at him long and hard. Arturo looked back at her, knowing the girl was looking at him like that because she was trying to reach the bottom of his look and that there, at the bottom of his look, was his grief and there was nothing for it but to stay there, quietly, so that the girl could see it. She moved her hands again, tidying the hair between his ear and temple. Very softly she said:

"You're hot for me, aren't you?"

Arturo wanted to grab the quilt and bury his hands in it. He wanted to say no, that it wasn't just that, that he wanted to be hot for her but also the same with her as her other friends, talking, doing things, getting together in a thousand ways. He wanted to say it, but his new skin had placed a silence on his lips and the same silence in his gaze. These were the eyes that offered her his grief. His grief moved his head. His grief nodded. The girl brought her moist tongue against his dry lips and pressed it against his teeth. Already Arturo could feel the pleasure of it in his stomach, in his thighs, in his hands which wanted to drown in her breasts and which were dizzy even before they brushed against them, in his prick which bulked magically. But his grief, instead of tensing him had decided for him that he should stay calm, and as her tongue passed his gums, mounted his own tongue, and wound round it within a delicious saliva, as her thin hands lightly scratched the roots of his hair, the nape of his neck, the first tremblings of his back, his hair began to stand up like the fur of a wild beast, and the more he held himself back, and the more he let himself go, the more his grief broke out and the deeper it plunged, and although he knew that he couldn't weep any more, his grief continued weeping, and when Susi opened his fly, eased out his cock with her slim fingers and already on top of him guided its tip saying to him, "put it into me", with only a fragile movement he was deep inside her and the girl wet his ear with saliva, calling him friend, and then Arturo knew that in his rapid ejaculation were the rest of the tears which his grief had left behind, and when they had all gone out of him between the walls of her belly which pressed against him pulsing like a heart, he said:

"I'm sorry. It's my first time."

And Susana fell onto his chest and sighed, nodding her head.

"It doesn't matter," she said.

He regarded Señor Pequeño, who was lying across the peasant track, and was obliged to shake him.

"Please, Dad. Don't go to sleep again. All this sleep will be bad for you."

The little man half-opened his eyes, and limited himself to arranging his head more comfortably on the crook of his arm.

"They'll all be after us soon," he yawned. "Look at those dogs. What are they waiting for?"

"You must come along with me, Dad. Trust me now. There's no other way."

"Trust you? Just wait until I wake up, and I'll take a stick to you."

"Don't let your eyes close, Dad. Get up."

"Not a chance." He jerked off his shoes, then held them aloft with his free arm. The sun filtered through the holes in the soles. "Look what you've done."

The Beast threw a stone to scare off a dog that had approached to sniff at his partner's feet. The mongrel drew back only a few yards, stretching out in the sun in an attitude of bored patience.

"I beg you, Señor Pequeño."

"Leave me here and be off with you. You've done me enough harm already. You and your whims, you and your coronary-producing surprises. Why didn't you tell me you had that flying number prepared. The food we could have eaten, the money we could have made!"

"Dad, you're fading away from us bit by bit. I don't know what you're talking about, I don't understand what you're saying, and all you do is lie there sleeping."

"No professionalism, amateur as ever."

The Beast shook him again, then parted his legs with a push of his hand. Señor Pequeño sat up on the track, hardly able to suppress another yawn.

"The dogs'll attack you and they'll chew you up whole. They'll gobble up your esteemed guts like vulgar noodles. Don't you realise?"

"I don't want that. I don't at all fancy the idea of those fangs in my neck."

"Get up then, Dad!"

He could only just keep his eyes open, and beckoned to the Beast to come over.

"Put your leg here, and I'll sleep a little siesta, then I promise we'll be off. If a dog comes along, kick it. How does that seem?"

Angel rubbed a thigh vigorously and let his partner position his head on it.

"Only five minutes," he said.

As the seconds passed, Señor Pequeño's body seemed to swell. As if fabricating a dream was the same for him as constructing a tower or a steel bulwark.

"Don't sleep too deeply, Dad, you're getting heavy. One of these days you'll turn into a corpse and I'll have to put you with the chicken."

His partner replied in a low murmur, and when the Beast lowered his ear to his mouth he could make out that he was speaking. It occurred to him then that Señor Pequeño could have made a fortune with this trick of dreaming and telling the dream at the same time. He thought of boxing him up in a gaily decorated coffin and touring the country fairs with a microphone inside the box and loudspeakers outside. If people with much less talent could write, spinning out words here and words there, then all the more could Señor Pequeño triumph, made up as he was of words from dreams like others are made up of bones.

He didn't even need to sit at a desk, like so many scribblers with no fire in their brains. All his partner would need was a comfortable coffin and a good microphone. That's how the Arab With the Smoking Mule had begun, and he'd become the owner of the Richmond Circus. What might not be the fruits, from the economic point of view, for example, of a Saturday morning with Señor Pequeño in the Vega Market?

At precisely that moment Señor Pequeño spoke:

"It's winter. I'm in a small house watching television. On the table is a square-patterned tablecloth edged with flowers."

"Yes, Dad."

"On the tablecloth is a vase full of violets. Beside the vase, hot soup which I have left there to cool."

"Good for you," said the Beast, noticing that the sun was beginning to set behind the hills.

"The television show is an operetta. Mario Lanza is singing. He's dressed as a bullfighter. There are slippers on my feet. Soft. Light. Stuffed with lambswool. A woman comes up to me and says: 'Ernesto, drink up your soup and go to bed. Tomorrow you have to get up early to go to work.' She says: 'I'm very happy they've given you a raise.'"

"Ernesto is a beautiful name, Dad. What is the house like? Does it have pink balconies?"

"I have a job."

"Big windows with blue frames?"

"I'm paid at the end of every month and invite my friends from the neighbourhood round to dinner. I have friends. I invite them round to dinner. Every month."

Angel went over to the ditch and formed a little container with his hands to carry back some water. He poured the water delicately over his partner's forehead and scattered it over his cheeks, lips and eyebrows. He propped Señor Pequeño's spine against the tree, and, kneeling down, tried to recreate the parting down the middle of his Gardelian coiffure.

"Might I ask what you think you're doing?" said the little man, without bothering to open his eyes completely.

"Trying to make you presentable, Dad. I want you to make a good impression."

"Did you make the parting good and straight?"

"Impeccable, Dad. There's a bit of dust on it, that's all." Then, as he shook him to get rid of both the dust and the dream, he bumped up against the bulk by his chest. "What have you got there?" He turned the inside pocket inside out, and the gun fell to the ground. "You could kill someone with that. Where did you steal it, Señor Pequeño?"

"The footballer gave it to me."

"Did you kill anyone, Dad?"

"I don't remember." Smitten with anxiety, the little man felt his forehead, his mouth and his cheeks. "By the way, you wouldn't happen to have a mirror you could lend me?"

"Father!"

"No, I'm not asking out of vanity. It's just that I've forgotten what I am."

Angel pushed the weapon into the props case and offered the other an arm to help him to his feet. Señor Pequeño hesitated for several seconds in front of the huge hand and said:

"I'm very tired. I'd like to take another nap."

The Beast leapt onto one of the dogs, caught it by the throat, pushed it in front of his partner's face and, thrusting his fingers into the animal's mouth, pulled its jaws apart until the saliva streamed from its fangs.

"Is this what you want, Señor Pequeño? To be eaten by these teeth?"

"Take them away, please. Look after me for five minutes while I doze off again."

"There's no more time, Dad. I have to get you away from here right now. The dogs and rats will attack after dark."

"I don't have it in me, don't you understand? Cursed be the day I joined forces with you. Haven't you realised my shoes have no soles?"

At which the Beast put his hands under the other's armpits and, bending down, swung him onto his back.

"What do you think you're doing?" the other protested.

"I'm going to carry you."

"Are you out of your mind? Think you're a bus now, do you?"

"Begging your pardon for asking you anything, Dad, but would you please stop kicking me in the kidneys as it's very painful."

From high above, Señor Pequeño saw the Beast was taking the path running alongside the ditch, and that in the distance there were street lamps and the lights of a town.

"I shall have my revenge," he said, accommodating his ear on the big man's shoulders. "I shall sleep deeply and dream a dream you'll not be able to bear. Your knees will give way and your spinal column will be damaged. I'll count to three before closing my eyes."

At that the Beast gestured upwards with his hand, both desperately and clumsily, warning:

"Dad!"

Señor Pequeño was meditating on the persistent irritation to his ear, deciding finally to investigate whether there was any blood.

"My own partner!" he said, before his hand made contact with his lobe.

When the woman opened the door and the deep dark of her eyes quickened the rest of her face with its sparkling, Señor Pequeño, as if lifted by an explosion, felt the thin film of his skin suddenly infused with blood. He thought the experience might even end in a smile, and only tore his gaze from the woman in black to see whether there was any glass nearby in which he could see his image reflected. He liked the lady's abundant, fleshy folds and the rouge-smoothed lips that shaped her mouth into a heart drawn by a child. She showed the tip of her tongue between rows of teeth that seemed much younger and fresher than the forty years with which she was coming juicily to ripeness. They remained caught up together on the threshold, motionless as at the end of a tango, the cloth of his trousers brushing against her sturdy knee, on to which fell the black miniskirt of her mourning, more like something from an advertising spot than widow's weeds.

"My *compadre*—my partner," said the Beast.

The couple's hands emerged simultaneously for the handshake as if someone were directing the scene.

"I'm Elvira," pronounced the woman in black, and Señor Pequeño heard other words within these, encased in the spoken syllables as within transparent plastic: my skin is as warm as a pillow where an adolescent has slept the night, my hair has the scent of honeysuckle and my breath is as fresh as a river, and I love a cup of wine when the moment is right, and I keep a good table with a tartan patterned tablecloth and flowers in a vase in the middle.

Señor Pequeño revealed the following:

"My name is Ernesto Lecaros. I consider myself a remarkably fortunate man, not because of past events in my life but because of this moment."

As if by suction, the widow's movement drew them

into the room, and without letting go of Señor Pequeño's hand she led him into the middle.

"I, exactly as you find me," said the widow, "am a qualified nurse."

"I have always admired medicine," said Señor Pequeño, parting his hand from her delicious fleshiness. The woman had not blinked once, and her constant smile could very well have been the copy of the one he felt had taken possession of his own face.

"Your smile, Señor Lecaros, is a marvel: contagious," said the woman, trying to reflect it in her own.

"It must be because it is brand new," said Señor Pequeño. "Today it has made its debut."

"It is truly original," she said.

"Oh, it's nothing." He looked at the Beast, who was also smiling away, his face infinitely soft. The big fellow winked very slowly at Señor Pequeño, who patted his slicked down hair once or twice and furtively fingered the corners of his lips. The woman continued to drink him in with an unyielding stare.

"This is my room," she said.

"I hardly know what to say. It pleases me immensely."

Already the widow's hand was on his wrist, and they walked a few yards as if floating on foam. She tugged at the cords of a small stage, like an altar on the plinth, surrounded artistically by lit candles. The shadows cast by the flames mingled on the white background cloth, forming endlessly fascinating figures.

"St Anthony," said the widow, her eyelashes as restless as the small shadows.

"Very miraculous," agreed the Beast.

"One of my favourite saints," declared Señor Pequeño.

The widow bit her knuckles, pulling at the skin with her impeccable little teeth.

"Life is made up of such coincidences," she declared.

When she turned round after closing the curtains, the two men did the same—and there it was. She neither pointed it out nor even looked at it. She contemplated the end of Señor Pequeño's chin as she spoke. As she said:

"And this is the bed."

Señor Pequeño poked out a finger and thrust it into the centre of the mattress with the precision of a surgeon.

"Seems very comfortable," he said.

The woman's lips suddenly seemed fleshier. Her small ears trembled as if the blood had difficulty in passing her temples.

"It is truly remarkable," she said, "how much you attract me."

Señor Pequeño studied the finger he had just pushed into the mattress, appearing to blow some indiscreet piece of fluff from it.

"Let's get on with it!" he whispered, overcome by a sudden huskiness.

"Do you mean it!" whispered the widow, her voice transformed suddenly into a sinuous purr. "I can't wait to embrace you. And—forgive my forwardness—to kiss you too, if at all possible."

Señor Pequeño drummed on the mattress, then slid his hand slowly over the quilt until diverting his fingers towards the shining lace of the pillow.

"Curious," he whispered, his voice almost gone. "You attract me as well."

"And I feel complete beside you. Like a cake with cream and candles. Indeed, if you wish to kiss me, or touch my breasts, or anything of the kind. . . ."

"Yes, yes, of course."

His lips advanced with the caution of a mountaineer, more closed than half-open, taking care to allow no immodesty to palpitate within his flesh. So it was her tongue which introduced itself like an animal into the cool intactness of his gorge. "This is cinema," he thought, trying to prevent his mind taking flight as the hot saliva of that heart-shaped mouth was impelling it to do. As his flesh opened he felt a new thirst for the moistness that he identified as lewdness. She was leaning on his shoulder, and in that position he could not see her passionate forehead. But he heard her words, which sounded to him like a reservoir of tears.

"Nobody has ever kissed me with such sweetness, not even my poor husband, who is with God in His Kingdom."

He kept his hand hanging free, as he wished to be discreet.

"It makes me very happy to know that you have no current commitments."

"Well, as you'll understand, I'm no virgin." Señor Pequeño blushed the colour of a *copihue* flower. "Excuse my frankness, but I've reached an age where I call a spade a spade. A man may be needed in this house, but never a pimp. No reference to you, of course."

"I understand."

"There's plenty of room here."

"To match your honesty, I'd like to say straight away that I intend to obtain work. Regular work with fixed pay."

The widow smiled at him for two intense minutes until he began to realise that her mouth was expanding as if full of fish and then the two of them smiled for another two minutes, until the widow placed a handkerchief over her breast and said:

"What about Angel?"

They walked to the front door and stood at the porch looking for him in complicitous silence.

"Seems as though my *compadre* has taken off,"
she said. "Maybe he's had the discretion to leave for
ever."

Señor Pequeño felt the perfect fit of the widow's
waist into his embrace, and that his fingertips could
even touch the lower part of her robust tits. His gaze
lost in the night, and nuzzling unceasingly against
his friend's body, he sighed, like a harp in flames:

"He was a faithful friend, but as an artist had his
ups and downs."

Only Corporal Sepulveda had made his excuses (declining the invitation for understandable reasons), but all of a sudden the whole neighbourhood was in the *pension* sawing up poles, scissoring away at banners, mixing paints, spreading butter and pâté on bread rolls, emptying Coca-Cola into urns, banging nails into wooden frames, sharing out the mimeographed broadsides, while on top of it all El Negro bounded from one group to another with his portable radio chirruping away that the Northern column was already passing the Plaza Artesanos, and that the Southern column was filing impressively past Che's statue and the flags were waving in the Don Tito Municipality like kites on fire, and this is just how it should be, Skinny, it's three years, three years it may be Negro but they've cost us balls, and the radio goes on counting up the demonstrators in hundreds of thousands, in Santiago alone there's getting on for a million of us, Mari, and two million'd be better just so's they know they'll not get it on a plate, and Don Manuel to the girls don't worry about dirtying the polish 'cos today is the Fourth, why don't we just sling the whole house out the window and we'll never forget this Fourth kids 'cos we're never gonna make it to the Eighteenth, and El Negro cool it Don Manuel what d'you want to depress the kids for (oi, belt up there's a good man, Skins, put a sock in it, don't get worked up, mate) don't you see Don Manuel the people are invincible there are millions of us how are they gonna kill all of us, and there must be some patriotic *milicos*, Don Manuel, don't say today of all days you've got a fit of the gloom-and-dooms, and Don Manuel no lad it's not that, it's just that I see you all here in my house like chicks in a dovecot and I don't want them to clip your wings when you're beginning to fly, my little spaniels, and El Negro but listen good to the radio Don Manuel, listen *the contingents are packed together like a calm sea with every wave saying we're here to be counted saying yes to justice saying yes to liberation saying yes president forward for our country and for Latin America a pure deep sea launched into the tide of history to wash away the crime of domination*, d'you hear, Don Manuel, *three irreversible years of revolutionary consciousness, and now our mines are ours, our copper is ours, the nitrate is ours, the iron is ours, the land is ours, the country is ours, president, happy birthday compañero presidente, happy birthday to all our people turned out into the streets with their banners with their brave youth with their helmets and their tools with their mothers with their girlfriends with their daughters smiling in the sun of this great festival for the country, yes to life they're saying, no to fascist murderers!* can you hear, Don Manuel, and let's form up, kids, into line with the women on the inside and the *compañeros* with the flags on either side, the banner up front, and the radio *here is the people saying support-support-the-people's-government, which is saying, ever-stronger, ever-stronger, ever-stronger, presidente*, girls, carry the sandwich bag, Mari, the drink urn, and let's get going for pete's sake they're saying the centre's full already that there's no room for a pin according to the radio, and the radio says *the victory will be won by uniting around the proletariat, the victory will be won by not letting the class become isolated, let them look and consider, look and consider, look and think and count us now, let them come and count us, hundreds of thousands, here we are present and for ever, unbeatable, señores coup-mongers, and the victory of the people means the unity of the patriotic soldiers with the revolutionary masses, with our people who don't want violence and who today are singing in the streets: you shall not pass; señores fascistas, our people, compañeros, are a human sea here in the city centre, and like our ocean it is fierce, tumultuous and endless though its name may be Pacific, take note, señores coup-mongers, go out onto the balcony and count us,* and El Negro says right, let's be off, for Chrissake *compañeros,* are we ready or not, everybody together, right we are, and El Negro are we in line or aren't we, and everybody, sure Negro we're in line, and sure Negro *venceremos,* and sure Skins let's get it together, and yes Don Manuel the country is stronger and now all of us in the street like a single lung *compañeros* like one person *compañeros* for our government's three years off we go together one two three: the-people-united-will-never-be-defeated, the-people-united-will-never-be-defeated, the-people-united-will-never-be-defeated, and louder, dammit, louder, and Skinny louder and Don Manuel louder and El Negro louder and louder the neighbours and louder everybody louder: the-people-united-will-never-be-defeated.

"Why wasn't my grandson there?"

The landlord blinked rapidly round the room.

"Your grandson?"

"Yes, señor, my grandson. The footballer."

Don Manuel changed his brush from hand to hand, and held out his right enthusiastically, after wiping it free of paint on his overall.

"Don't tell me you're Arturito's Grandad!"

The old man gripped his hand and let it fall after giving it a brief shake.

"Can you tell me why my grandson didn't go?"

Still holding on to his suitcase, the old man looked like a weathercock spinning in the middle of the room. Don Manuel pointed towards the stairs.

"He may be in his room."

"Unfortunately, you know, he's my only grandson. I'll go and look for him."

"Upstairs and to the left."

His long nervous strides made short work of the staircase, and in front of the first door he let go of the suitcase's weight, making it bounce violently against the wall.

"Grandad!" The youth leapt off the bed, the book still in his hand, his arms already measured for the embrace, a smile already spilling over his cheeks. Susana was finishing sewing the star on her armband, and the shock of the blow at the door made her prick herself with the needle. The old man's arms reached downwards like a fortification or the severe frontier of a country. Inches from him Arturo was left with only the empty form of his embrace.

"One thing at a time!" His Grandad skewered him with the phrase, and in a single movement snatched the book left hanging at the end of his pointless embrace. "What's this you're reading?" With his eyebrows stormy, he scrutinized the volume of Neruda's poems like a cardsharp ventilating the cards before shuffling them and enclosing them again in his hand. "Fine!"

"Grandad."

"One thing at a time."

"Grandad, let me introduce you to Susana."

The old man walked over to the girl, and for a second allowed a fleeting sweetness to break through his harshness. Though he made sure that Arturo didn't catch a glimpse. His handshake with the girl was instantaneously that of old comrades, old mutually needed cronies. As if sensing this, Arturo wanted at least to put his arm round his shoulder, so as to be included. But once again his Grandad, as if executing a tango step, gave a tiny shrug of his shoulders, and left him out of step.

"One thing at a time." He pointed a finger at the centre of his grandson's chest. "Are you still a virgin, or is that settled?"

Arturo felt as if nobody in history had ever blushed as deeply as he at that accursed moment. The old man flashed a smile that revealed his empty gums, and with the same smile on his face stared unblinkingly at Susana.

"I ...," said the youth.

"Never mind! A good eye, few words needed!" Puffing out his neck, he attempted a particularly ferocious posture. "Third thing: are you a man of the left?"

The youth shrugged his shoulders.

"Dunno, Grandad." He gestured towards the girl.

"What d'you mean, you don't know?"

"I don't know, Grandad."

Susana ostentatiously pinned on the armband and stood up.

"Grandad," she smiled, "what Arturo needs...."

"Balls! That's what he needs!" He lifted the quilt covering the old felt sofa and scratched a finger along its surface. "Very well. Tonight I'll sleep on this heap. Right now I'm off to the march with the people." He bent his elbow and offered it to Susana. "Are you going too, señorita?"

The girl tossed her hair, and fitted her arm into his with a courtesan's thrust, like a great lady. Together, they looked at Arturo.

"Seriously, aren't you coming?" she said.

The youth rubbed his legs. The two of them looked to him like poor but happy kings, breathing easily, haloed by a sudden glory. He felt their freshness had also moistened him a little, but in his tense mouth the energy of his marvellous grief had not yet done its work.

"I would go," he murmured, "but...."

And he opened his hands like an ungainly bird, revealing himself, alone, and Fats with his split mouth against the wall.

"What's on your mind, friend?" she said, softly, delicately, ruffling the edges of his thoughts, as if secretly humming the same song. The couple left the room like a bride and bridegroom on their wedding day, carried away in a soft fever.

The lad couldn't resist following them a short distance behind, and from the third stair waited for them to go out of the front door, then plunged his hands into his pockets like someone who has watched the jet plane carrying an impossible love disappear on a far journey. For the first time the *pension* displayed a perfect silence, filled from wall to hospitable wall with leftovers, sawdust, chips from wooden frames, red banners mixed up with the ballerinas, the president, vases swollen with violets, tall lilies, the piano dark as a piece of night on the rustic patchwork carpet. "Home," said his grief. He caressed the bannister down to the bottom step and touched the polished decoration in which it ended, a kind of carved pine-nut over whose undulations his fingers could wander as if through the wavy hair of a hippy girl. He played the highest notes of the piano, searching for a simple melody to match that silence a little or one of those poems by Neruda peopled by girls with berets and trembling thighs. As if it were the natural continuation of the keyboard he picked up from the rim of the instrument an armband similar to the one Susana had been sewing in his room while comforting him with that way she had of tidying his hair, and telling him that there was love to be found in many places, that if it couldn't be here then there'd be someone else, more beautiful, better than me, Arturo, and what happened happened that once, that's all, and don't build false hopes, keep hold of it if you like or forget it, but don't carry on like that begging for what can't be for you, Arturo, talented as you are, and so on. And he had traced the lines of a poem word by word with his finger, but there was no such sweetness in his mouth, he was still far from the country where such words join and weave, where such phrases fuse and sing and murmur with the same rhythm with which he'd known how to breathe in the bed in Susana's house while the old lady scratched at the door, open for me, my girl, open for me.

"Home," his grief repeated, among the ashtrays overflowing with ash, olive stones, leftover mortadela, dead butts and old newspapers where the kids had tried out the black, red and yellow for the streamers. He went over to the mirror and contemplated his own relaxedness, his neck gently cocked, and the armlet held at the end of his fingers. He peered into himself, wanting his face to be as decipherable as a book where the story of his life was written and he had only to read it and follow it like a script. And even though there might be mistakes, falls, and painful episodes written there, they would be his own, as deeply his own as his bones or his liver. He bent his left arm, and without taking his eyes from the mirror fitted the elastic of the armband perfectly onto his forearm. He flexed, and the symbol squeezed tighter against him as the muscle expanded. He moved his lips and, absorbed in himself, heard the words as if spellbound by his own reflection.

"*Compañero*," he heard gently, like the ebb of a peaceful sea.

"*Compañero*," he said.

"*Compañero*," the voice sang, now full-bodied, deep, and in the edge of the mirror appeared the image of Fats, his arm strapped against his jacket and covered with multicoloured plaster.

Arturo spun round, and confronted the whole of Fats' grin, there in the centre of the room, just a little proud of his arm, as if he were a wounded and victorious Napoleon, exactly like the pictures in history books. Arturo felt as if he'd been caught naked in the toilet and with a confused grimace tried uselessly to cover the armlet with his hand. He held his fingers there while embarrassment flooded his mouth.

"Fats," he said.

Fats took in the silence as if it were the first time he'd heard it. He noticed the silent piano, the aged carpets, the scattered rubbish.

"Looks like they've gone, eh?"

"Just now." He swallowed. "Did they bugger your arm?"

Fats sized up the plaster cast as if it were a rare novelty.

"Yup. They thought they'd have a go at me." Arturo had lowered his hand a little, and Fats briefly eyed the armband. "So, they've gone then."

"Yeah, they've all gone."

"Recently, though."

"Sure, just now."

The two of them stayed rooted there, pointlessly fingering at different parts of their bodies as if for lack of cigarettes between their fingers. Arturo pointed with his chin at the region in plaster.

"Hurt much?"

"Not any more. Look." Arturo stepped forward a couple of paces and, with a slight grimace of pain, Fats managed to lift the piece of his jacket that lay over the plaster. Now Arturo could see clearly that the multicoloured gaity of the cast was due to its

203

being painted all over with the symbols of all the left-wing parties. "Had a great time in hospital. The kids from the union came and thought it'd be a laugh to decorate this bugger. Look at the red there and the green with the little star over there and the Christians' sky-blue one there. What d'you reckon?"

"Looks great on you, man."

"It's a gas when they plaster you, see."

"A gas," said Arturo, hearing the simple sincerity, unadorned and unqualified, with which a second before Fats had said it's a gas, watching Fats' face with its little splinter of chain stuck in his mouth and the white bandage fixed to his cheek, hearing also his own grief, his own pure lack of words.

"Anyway, must be getting along."

"Sure," said Arturo, and they stayed there motionless waiting for the boat to weigh anchor, as if Fats had only just arrived and they had to strike up conversation. Fats studied the tips of his shoes and curled and uncurled his toes.

"So, there's absolutely nobody here?"

"Nobody."

Arranging his jacket over the plaster once again, Fats stood nodding his assent with the point of his chin.

"Bye, then," he said.

"Bye, Fats."

He watched the other's bulk move off towards the door with the caution of the wounded, stout, a body without a skeleton, the rump of an all-suffering and enduring horse, and when he had almost reached the door Arturo's grief cried out:

"Fats!"

He saw him turn with his huge eyebrows raised and a smile that seemed indelible, the very image of what Fats was deep inside, amiable, inquiring, calm, a perfectly serene, deep lake, and he found himself beside him without noticing the steps that took him there. He tore off his armband, and stretching the elastic to its limits, invited Fats to offer him the plaster so he could fit it over it. Osorio's eyes stayed lost in the wall as Arturo carried out the operation. Only when the lad had stepped back to admire the band over the whole set of emblems, did he look back at him, smiling the same as ever.

"That's what was missing, Fats," said the youth.

"Are you crazy, son. It's yours!"

But because by now all the water in the lake had soaked him deeper than even his own breath had ever reached, Arturo took a deep breath and, a warm and darting smile opening between his teeth, higher-flying than a seagull, let himself and his sadness reply in unison:

"No."

if you want something from me, *compañero*, just say
I was born again, born in reverse like a corpse, that
instead of coming out of my mother's belly I came
out from inside that humiliating shadow, that was
how I came out of the Stadium, look at these fingers
and take note of these ribs, tell me how my eyes are
now, you who knew them before, and sure, no names,
just between you and me, in silence, because it's no
longer like it was before when every house was a fiesta,
and all sounds a celebration and the nights endless
conversation, and they say all that was hatred, but
tell me what this is then, tell me please what this is
now because they said that was all hatred, that your
*compadre* El Negro was hatred, that Fats was, that
Mari and Susana were, and I ask how, and maybe you
can tell me, maybe you can advise me, what is all this,
what country is this: and you'll remember how it was
before and spell it out to me, maybe you'll tell me that
some time then I was alive and there was a piano in
my house instead of this shadow, although the shadow doesn't hurt as much as remembering, as much
as being here with you privately, with this silence like
a plague, tell, if you like, how a dead man talks, how
death ate me up bit by bit and left me as you see me
now, you who know who I am, if you can call the person talking to you anyone, and everybody talks
about the planes because of the marks they leave and
everybody talks about the tanks because you can see
the walls and the ashes from the fires and the stomachs slashed open by bullets and the corpses in the
river like silent logs, sure, you can see that, you can

touch it, you can wound yourself a thousand times over remembering all that, but talk to me about this other death, tell me, then go way over there and repeat what I'm telling you now, tell them about the funerals, tell them how dismal the air is, how squalid our hands and necks are, like shipwrecked boats, how the smiles on the mouths are the final spasms of screams, of vomiting, of cries and why do you want me to go like a corpse among other corpses, cadavers that breathe, for a whole month we were as ashamed of carrying on living as of dying, of dying of old age, with the whiskers of our beards befuddling our tongues, legs stiff with tedium, stomachs empty and the cash for the tipple in the corner bar and the sun coming in as if to shatter itself against the piano, tell them about this other death I'm telling you about, tell it without the planes flying over its head or the tanks crushing it or the machine guns that scared off the birds, the burned dust made off with them, the ones who disappeared, the nests blown around on the sidewalks, what do you want me to tell you, between you and me tell them this, that it was worse than death, until we get reorganized, tell them that, all of them, say I don't recognise this country, though I was born here, yes say that, ask them what all this means, there's the *cordillera* and so what? there's the sun and so what? the clouds and so what, the house and so what, do they think I'm an animal, that they're going to drug me with dogs' bones and their solemn faces and crossed legs, do they think I was born dead, that I don't remember that I was happy, what tenderness was, the music and the night we went out on the porch to watch the stars and walked down the street like one person, tell them that over there, do they think forgetfulness gets written in the newspapers, tell them that rage is burying its nails in our stomachs, that a beaten back hurts more when the club is silent, when you can hear the radios, all those whores dolled up like ladies, slavering, false teeth, all of them out there, the whores with their rotten teeth their tongues and their military marches one two three, and I don't know, señor, *compañero*, it's not possible, and even if I'm wrong a thousand times over I tell you this isn't my country, I never knew this before, I don't understand it, I never saw a bullet in my life and now I have three deaths weighing on me, and more than that I don't know, I only know that many have gone to another country, a country where death is so perfect that there's no longer any air or sun or mouths or tongues or saliva or blood, that's the country they want, a happy copy of death the same slavering silence, necks on the floor, eyes in the street searching out for boots and escape, spooks, the pecks of vultures, and it was only on Monday that Fats had his plaster off, the way things happen, Don Manuel, he said to me, when he set off for the factory, they take off my armour just as the war is starting, and with my luck they'll put a bullet through my hide now, and El Negro was already ringing the bell, I'd bolted the door, *compañero*, I don't know why, see, things were still normal in the house, and when I opened up the first artillery blasts came in with El Negro, and you could see the tanks jolting along like hell and El Negro says hello *compañeros*, impeccable he was, El Negro, stiff as a head waiter, freshly shaved and a newspaper folded under his arm, and he says not to get alarmed because they were police armoured cars and the people were cheering them in the streets because they say they're loyal and they're going to defend the palace and once again he says not to get alarmed that we stopped them once before and with God's help we'll stop them again, ain't that right, Fats? sure, that's right and Fats let's go El Negro, and hang on a bit I said feeling a kind of premonition, wait a bit, lads, don't go out, wait and see what happens, you never know what you may find in your way, what you might come across in the district, and El Negro pulls out his paper from his armpit and opens it wide so I can read the headline and the paper says in fat red letters as clear as you like that everyone had to be where it was their duty to be, in the posts they'd been allotted, and he told me that if everyone waited to see what happened before doing anything, when we did move it would be straight into clandestinity, even so, lads, I said, it's not for the sake of saying it, wait here a bit longer, wait until the *compañero* speaks over the radio again, wait because Sepulveda said he'd call me (did Sepulveda call, Don Manuel, did he? did he?), he'll tell us how things really are, the *compañero* said we shouldn't let ourselves be massacred, son, the *compañero*, El Negro interrupted me, is where he should be while we're still fucking about here, look *compañero*, now that you ask me, why shouldn't you tell about the tanks and the planes and count the bullets and the corpses, seeing as how you ask me what it was I felt, the way I felt it, well it was like this, I should tell you that El Negro seemed to me like a saint floating in the air, it struck me that he was as pure and proud as a kite in September, I felt ashamed saying to him what I said, I felt ashamed saying and what if we lose? because I felt it was like spitting in the font, and El Negro stared at me, that's all, reproachful-like, if you follow me, El Negro said to me, and I'll never forget it because he called me *Manuelito*, Manuelito, he says, we're invincible; and I saw the two of them standing there as strong as trees, not a bit of nerves, El Negro all serious, because El Negro, well you hardly knew him, went about thinking about politics all day, about getting things organised, so that nothing should ever go wrong, cheering up the *compañeros* when they got depressed when the *fachos* kept

knocking us about, and Fats like always, his arm
crooked inside the gauze they'd given him to replace
the plaster, calm as you like, as if he hadn't a worry in
the world, Fats, as if he only had to go out onto the
sidewalk and a regiment of patriotic soldiers would
be waiting for his orders, that's how El Negro smiled
at me and thats how Fats looked at me, and maybe it
doesn't mean anything to you, but they've stayed for
ever afterwards in my head, the two of them together
as if joined by the wind, the both of them, my Negro
and my Fats, forgive me for talking to you like this
'cos maybe it's not what you were interested in hearing, between you and me let's talk straight, and I
have a sentimental deviation, as the kids say, and
that's about the size of it, if you understand me, and
anyway that was the last time I saw El Negro, and I
don't know what else you want to know, can I offer
you anything, some wine, coffee

what I know I know, and any more than that I can't
tell you, forgive me that it's so little but sometimes I
get the feeling it has all been gone over too much,
that it all rolled over the days like an enormous eraser
and wiped them out, and just two or three things are
left, El Negro and Fats standing there, the call from
Sepulveda, or rather the call from his *compadre*, the
shootout here, all that, but now it's as if they all
mount up on top of me at once, and I can't separate
one from the other, neither what happened before nor
what happened afterwards, you're a sensitive person
and you'll understand what it is I'm trying to tell you,
after all at the end of the day writing is your calling,
while mine, God knows what it was, what it should
have been, although now I think I know, except I
couldn't tell

no, I swear to you I couldn't, it's as if my calling
now should be to die, to do something really important and let them flay me with their bullets, but Fats

is Fats and he convinced me not to, and I'm about as soft over them as a dog over its pups, do you get me? it happens sometimes that you find that instead of the kids looking like their dad the dad looks like the kids, you came out just like your boy, old man, haven't you ever heard that? and when all's said and done it's very fine what you're doing and I'm sorry I've had to tell you nothing but sad things, like I have to tell you that El Negro's dead, that they killed my Negro more or less an hour after they killed the *compañero* Presidente, they shot him from a helicopter in the backyard of the factory, the bullets smashed him into the floor tiles, and Fats says that only his face was left whole, not a scratch, the same El Negro just as if he was alive, as if he'd just finished doing any job, school homework or something, says Fats, anything other than dead, and if that's how he says it was then that's how it was, because Fats saw him, and sure I begin to think about the way things are, that everyone has so much to weep over after what they saw but I didn't see anything of how they murdered my Negro, and it grieves me to think that if I suffer so much when I think about it then what must Fats feel who saw it with his own eyes, Fats who wanted to take El Negro's body out to the neighbourhood and bury it anywhere, dig a hole for it in the square, so as not to leave him for the trucks that they brought round to cart away the bodies, he didn't want El Negro to disappear for the last time like a cloud that just passes over and is gone, but he couldn't carry him, the *compañeros* said he was crazy, by then there were only five of them left, or was it six he told me? and they'd decided to abandon the factory, that it had been agreed, they said, that they shouldn't let themselves be massacred, and finally they got through to them by phone, that they had to get out of there, cross the township and go to the metal factory, the resistance was serious there, that they should keep their spirits up the *compañeros* because if the *compañero* had died it was because he wanted to leave us an example of how to be true to yourself, and right now *compañeros*, they told them, being true to ourselves means keeping hold of the factories which we knew how to make our own and death is a small price, *compañeros*, that's what Fats says the *compañero* said, and they went through the township, where everyone was running from house to house, the planes were buzzing them and buses and tanks were beginning to surround them, and they said the soldiers were going to come in shooting as if closing a circle and no one was going to be let off, that the soldiers were saying they should go out one by one to the buses, and Fats says the local *compañeros* said they weren't stupid, no way would they leave, that those who were leaving were being shot there and then, that there was nothing for it but to scupper out the back or hang on until the shooting was over, that any two corpses look much alike, but it's much better to die putting up a fight than doing nothing, dead through surrendering or keeping quiet, and so they had to get out and well, you hardly knew El Negro you say, but the sad fact is that El Negro was left there, in the yard, with all the bullets inside him, and we never saw him again, do you see? because the pits were deep and dug for hundreds, understand?

and I don't know what else to tell you, ever since I knew El Negro was dead it's as if the house got bigger, I spent hours looking at how far away the walls seemed to grow, and sometimes nothing could move me from this chair and Juana would pass by sweeping the fluff off that carpet as if nothing had happened, as if we were going to be twelve at table instead of me on my tod like a lone candle not wanting to try even a piece of lettuce, stirring my soup, that's right, *compañero*, since El Negro and Sepulveda died I've felt as if I was redundant too, the hours were nothing but cups of coffee without a single thought in my head, because don't imagine I spent my time here thinking, it's simply that if you look at the piano the house grows bigger and your heart shrinks smaller, and to look at it there now who'd imagine those keys used to play the most glorious waltzes, how could you imagine it if even I who knew Sepulveda well can hardly do so, who would imagine that when the telephone rang early on the Wednesday it wouldn't be Sepulveda who'd sworn to ring but someone who said Don Manuel, you don't know me and it's better that way, and me who can this be, what bad news are they going to hit me with now, because many had died for the first time over that phone, best if I don't even remember, and the voice says, Don Manuel I'm Sepulveda's *compadre* and you don't know me but I know you by reputation, Don Manuel I know that you and Sepulveda got on fine, and well, I don't know, I'm calling to give you some bad news, and I'd already guessed what that sad news would be, it seemed that the telephone was black because the shitty thing knew some day we were all going to start dying, as if the bastard knew that a September like this would come along no? with all those lungs punctured by bullets and the sky rotten with cannon blasts and the birds crumpled on the sidewalks, the sadness inside me had no limits, *compañero*, the sad news, Don Manuel, said the *compadre*, is that they've shot Sepulveda, the bastards shot my *compadre* right there in the station, my *compadre* who never fired a shot in his life died from a bullet, you don't know me Don Manuel and this is all I've got to tell you, I know you respected Sepulveda and as far as I'm concerned he died as naive as ever because he was the only one who stepped forward, the only one among all of them who thought like him, to show his brown face, always perfectly shaved, impeccable, and his sleepy eyes, Don Manuel, he stepped forward, he did it without any fear, without any fuss, without thinking anything of it, he did it because that was Sepulveda, innocent, nobody in the world better than my *compadre*, and right there the lieutenant did away with him with a bullet, you know who's talking to you don't you? he said, his *compadre*, Sepulveda's *compadre*, you know? I'm letting you know because of the room, okay? in case you want to rent it, see? maybe I'll see you later, maybe I'll call in, but now you know, so look after his things, his radio, I don't know, and that's how the corporal's *compadre* called me and here I am at your service if there's anything else it occurs to you I can help you with, anything I may have left out, anything else you may be curious about, it's still early and there's no danger you'll be caught by the curfew, and if you are, you can stay and sleep here if you want to take the risk after all they're all vacant, from one to fifteen, the only thing alive here is the dust, I'll never clean again, never sweep again, there's only silence occupying the rooms here, thick as ice that never melts, which is everywhere, it touches you wherever you go, a filthy silence, full of bullets, like those in the distance, can you hear them? can you hear them? can you hear them closer now? do you know them? stay if you want to, feel at home, if you want to risk it, sure, can you hear them now? can you hear them? it was one of those that killed my Angel, *compañero*, a big fellow, tall, as good as you could wish for the poor lad, he went kind of crazy, about fifteen of them came looking for Fats Osorio, a whole busload of them came up the street, bristling with everything you can imagine, rifles, machine guns, they began to spread out like an oil stain, they spread out through the whole block, and Fats said to me, well Don Manuel looks like my number's up, this is the bum's rush for your Fats and what can we do for him, and there was precious little time left before they'd ring the bell, and we could see everyone inside now holding bullets in their hands, sharing out the bullets like toys, and it was then that Angel came down the stairs with a revolver, carrying the revolver in his fist as if it was a flag, comes over to me and says Señor Fats don't give yourself up they'll kill you like they killed El Negro, they'll kill you like they killed Señor Sepulveda, run away and I'll cover you, and Fats says don't be crazy Angelito, put that away, and we could already imagine the lieutenant's face in the house, put that bugger away, Angelito, that won't get us anywhere, don't you see, and Angel ran away through the yard Señor Osorio I'll defend you with this, and I say to him, run Fats for God's sake if you don't run they'll kill the lot of us, they'll shoot us to pieces and I'm pushing Fats out through the door to the yard, and I take him out to the henhouse and from there open the door to the liquor store garage and call the owner and he's a good sort and straightaway hides Fats on the floor of his truck and says to him we'll be well out of this before they get here and when I get back I don't know what to tell you because they were all in the lounge with Angel on the floor as dead as a clod of earth, with a tiny hole in his chest, as if they knew they were shooting a child, there he was Angel a small *cordillera* they'd brought down with a single pinprick, he was laid out smiling, as if they'd offered him wine instead of a bullet, had lifted the cup to Angel's maw, his lips always trembling like a rabbit's, you didn't know him very well did you, right, and really maybe he was right because he wanted everyone to call him the Beast, but I never called him that, out of respect, do you see? although he might laugh, although he might laugh, I who only knew him slightly don't know who he was and so what can I tell you, if you take a photograph of the house it won't show the silences, it won't show that new silence that Angel brought to the house, a mute thing as big as him which maybe you can't even make out, Angelito died bigger than a piano and me with the *milicos* there in front of me I couldn't believe they already had him dead, with one little bullet it was, one blow, one single shot like an arrow, kind of soft and Angel's face as if they had sent him floating away, just as if a cloud of red wine had lifted him up high and far away, what words can I use to say who Angel What's-his-name was, he never signed me a receipt because he never paid a penny, he never had a single note by his own efforts to get happy with, he was the worst piece of business I'd done since I opened the *pension* after tiring of so much travelling the world, so much watching people buy and sell buy and sell, I can say that Angel's pocket left the *pension* unvanquished and on top of that he could have cost me the price of his funeral because the lieutenant pointed to him there, right where you're looking, and says to me now you can look after the burial because we're not about to become undertakers, sure that's what he said at the same time as the machine gun was stuck in my kidney and the one with the machine gun took me out into the street with my hands in the air, hands in the air he threw out into the street and that's where I stayed the whole night, thinking to myself they're all dead all of them, the streets nothing but sticky blackness and the *milicos* standing there smoking under the streetlamp, and one of them says to me hands in the air you're under arrest and here's another customer for the Stadium, let's see if they'll play a match with him before we kick him into goal full of lead, and I say to a sergeant but sergeant, who's going to bury Angel who's left there dead on the carpet, when Juana Gomez sees him there she'll drop dead too, you can't do that, and the lieutenant said I was to stay behind to bury him, and the sergeant said not to worry that if I was ever to come back some day the cats will have eaten this Angelito you're talking about and let's get moving to the Stadium, and there I'd be able to count the resistance, and who did I think I was, mine was the only house in the neighbourhood where there'd been any resistance, then he started on about me having a Spanish accent and whether I'd been in the Spanish Civil War and if I'd fucked any nuns, that's what they asked me in the bus, and they were already beating me in the ribs with their rifle butts, nothing too heavy yet, in the bus they were blows as if to say "we're hitting you, gently, but we're hitting you", and that's my story and here I am still alive as they say, help yourself to wine, make yourself at home, help yourself, when your mouth is full of corpses your tongue gets rough, now can you feel the silence, can you? I don't know if it's just in my head or whether you notice it too, that's the silence that has damned this house since they killed Angel there on that carpet and don't go any closer because any nearer you'll see the blood, it's pink now, sure, because Juana washed the carpet with detergent and I realise you don't want to hear about these practical ordinary things and I don't think I know what else to tell you, you can see how I'm settled here with the silence and Juana Gomez who cooks what she can, what the *compañeros* give us from here and there, and don't even ask about Juanita Gomez because to begin with it was as if the silence had killed her even while she was still alive, her lips went purple and she walked through the rooms shivering, which is why I let her sweep, to warm her up a bit, that's why between you and me and don't repeat it I let her look for the foreign stations to tune into at night, and that's how she's been, lips purple and trembling and her ear lowered to the receiver and when it talked about us she'd signal with a finger and put another to her lips and listen and nod agreement and cough with her hands over her mouth because since they killed El Negro, and Sepulveda, and Angel, and since my brother who owns the taxi went to look for Carlitos who they say they're holding prisoner in a nitrate camp in the north, Juana's had a cough that never lets up, and I think she coughs so much because she speaks so little, and since she never cries the most likely is that it's nerves I reckon without knowing anything about medical matters, that's to say I guess if you stay inside with all this sure you cough or something, feel as if you're going to suffocate, and maybe that cough is a way of defending herself I reckon, sure, to begin with we talked a bit, about the shopping for example, or having no money, or if it would rain or not, you know, things like that, except once when she told me what she'd like to do, and you're the only person I've told this to, that she'd discovered that she would learn to live for the sake of one single thing, and I asked her what it was that had turned her so mysterious and complicated when she'd always been so direct, simple, with few words, so that I should understand clearly, and she told me it was to be alive for when once again we'd have another march like that tremendous one down the Alameda and El Negro and Angel would be there, the both of them would be there as well, and she knew they'd be carrying flags and there'd be so many millions in the streets that not even God would be able to count them even though He had as many fingers as there are stars in the sky and El Negro and Angel's flags would cover the whole street like a banner, a great sheet bigger than a cloud, and that's the reason she'd stay alive, and that's what Juana told me the only time we talked, and I said but Juana, how can you say that my dear when you saw Angel dead at your feet, don't you remember, how he stayed there for ever as if he'd been embalmed, I asked her are you crazy Juanita, that I didn't want to disappoint her but Negro and Angel are dead I said, couldn't she hear the silence in the house like a volcano, couldn't she see the empty table and the dust on the piano, and Juana Gomez looked at me as if laughing at me, just as if I was a child who'd played a prank on her, put her hands between her legs like I'm showing you and moved her head very slightly and wagging her finger like a primary school mistress explained that I shouldn't get things mixed up, Don Manuel, that I shouldn't be taken in by details, that El Negro and Angel weren't dead, but on a special mission, that they'd gone to heaven to receive instructions for a march where for every person there'd be a star and that they would come back from heaven wrapped in a banner so big its tail would trail along the *cordillera* like a comet, and that's all she was living for, and *compañero* Fats didn't die so he could go on resisting and let them know from here on earth when they should come down with the banner, and that's why *compañera* Susana was still alive, and why *compañera* Mari was still alive, and she said Don Manuel, how much longer are we going to stay here sweeping the carpet, you're sitting there as if you were the corpse and not *compañero* Negro, how long are we going to stay here as mute as two armchairs, Don Manuel, we've been wandering about choked with death for long enough, and then she switched off the radio and said Don Manuel, dear boss of mine, Don Manuel, we have to get organised, and that's the lot I reckon that I have to tell you, our lives changed a lot from then on, and about Juana Gomez and all that, I reckon that's all I know

*and here we are*
*more than that I cannot say*
*you'll understand compañero*
*'cos if you open your mouth the flies get in*
*and the parrot's big mouth was the end of him*

"That's fine, Don Manuel," I said. "Thanks for the wine and your trust in me. There was only one other thing I wanted to ask. What became of the footballer and his Grandad?"

"They detained young Arturo on September 24 at the poet's funeral. Now he's with his Grandad in the south. I can tell you they're fine, and hope that's enough."

"But do you ever see them, or write, or talk to them?"

"That's all I know."

"So that's about it."

"That's right."

"Well, thanks anyway."